CLASSIC GHOST STORIES

Edited by Molly Cooper
Illustrated by Barbara Kiwak

Lowell House
Juvenile
Los Angeles

CONTEMPORARY BOOKS
Chicago

To my parents,
who passed their love of the classics down to me
—M. A. C.

To Lynn, for her wonderful support and encouragement
—B. K.

ISBN: 1-56565-279-7

Library of Congress Catalog Card Number: 95-21101

Publisher: Jack Artenstein
Vice President/General Manager, Juvenile Division: Elizabeth Amos
Editorial Director: Brenda Pope-Ostrow
Director of Publishing Services: Rena Copperman
Project Editor: Barbara Schoichet
Managing Editor, Juvenile Division: Jessica Oifer
Art Director: Lisa-Theresa Lenthall
Typesetting: Laurie Young

Lowell House books can be purchased at special discounts when ordered in bulk for premiums and
special sales. Contact Department JH at the following address:
Lowell House Juvenile
2029 Century Park East, Suite 3290
Los Angeles, CA 90067

Manufactured in the United States of America

10 9 8 7 6 5 4 3 2 1

Some of the entries in this collection have been abridged.

Contents

CLASSIC GHOST STORIES
Introduction

Dear Reader:

Have you ever thought you put something somewhere, only to find it someplace else? Have you ever glimpsed a person going by and looked behind you to find no one there? The thought sends a chill down your spine, makes you think that maybe, just maybe, there might be such a thing as ghosts. Though your rational self scoffs at such thoughts of spirits, specters, and spooks, still, you can't seem to dismiss them . . . entirely.

There are many names for phantoms and just as many ways to describe the world in which they roam. But whether one calls that creepy cosmos the afterlife or the "other world," it definitely is a place that has had people pondering for centuries.

Like people, ghosts have personalities ranging from playful to petrifying. Some are harmless, even gentle—just lost souls looking for a way to escape the misery they experienced on Earth. Some are nothing more than a presence, choosing, for some unknown reason, to enter the lives of strangers to whom they somehow feel connected. And some are frightening phantoms, returning to Earth to wreak havoc on those who wronged them in their wretched lives. All play a role in the subconscious—or is it the *conscious?*—mind, which is forever wondering what happens when we leave our earthly bodies and enter the unknown world beyond.

Now, here for your contemplative pleasure, are some of the most macabre offerings of the masters of fright. Prepare yourself to encounter a host of horrifying haunts, undead spirits, and lost souls as you enter the world of **CLASSIC GHOST STORIES**. Full of eerie excerpts and supernatural short stories written by literature's masters of horror, this treasury of timeless tales will bend your mind with wondrous works that have long outlived their famous authors.

So . . . do you dare to turn the page? Do you?

The Furnished Room

by O. Henry

No one could say O. HENRY'S *life was uneventful. En route to
becoming one of the most recognizable names in literature, he held
a number of jobs as far removed from writing as could be, including
that of a rancher, a bookkeeper, and a bank teller. But what most people
don't know about this famous author, who was born on September 11,
1862, in Greensboro, North Carolina, is that his real name was
William Sydney Porter, and that he also spent some time in prison!*

*After dropping out of school at the age of fifteen, O. Henry went to
work in his uncle's drugstore. But it wasn't until 1882, when
O. Henry moved to Texas, that his real adventures began. There, he
met Athol Estes, whom he eloped with in 1887. Later, in 1895, at
the age of thirty-three, he first broke into print when The Daily Post, a
newspaper in Houston, Texas, published his short stories "Tales of the
Town" and "Some Postscripts."*

*But how did O. Henry end up in prison? It all began when
O. Henry was summoned to stand trial for the embezzlement of funds
from the First National Bank where he had been a teller. On his way
back to Austin for the trial, it seems he caught a train going to New
Orleans instead. From there, he headed for Honduras, where he met and
befriended the famous outlaw brothers, Al and Henry Jennings, who*

had stolen $30,000 in a bank robbery. The three men then used that money to travel around South America.

But in 1897 O. Henry got word that his wife was seriously ill, and after returning to Austin, he was sentenced to five years in prison. During this time he wrote several short stories and acquired the pen name that remains with him today. The exact origin of the name O. Henry is still unknown, but it might have come from Orrin Henry, who was a prison guard, or from a French pharmacist, Etienne-Ossian Henry, who wrote a reference work that O. Henry used while serving out his prison term.

When he left prison in 1901, after shortening his sentence for good behavior, O. Henry moved to his beloved New York, where the bulk of his stories were written. In 1907 he married his second wife, Sarah Lindsay Coleman. Unfortunately, however, he contracted tuberculosis three years later and died in a hotel room on June 5, 1910.

O. Henry produced over six hundred works in his lifetime, creating a specific style and method that were to become his trademark. Most notable was his habit of ending stories with an ironic twist. This trait appears again in "The Furnished Room," where a young man, desperately searching for his beloved, never realizes that his search could be over—if only he could know the spine-tingling secret that is within the four walls where he is staying.

Restless, shifting, fugacious as time itself is a certain vast bulk of the population of the red brick district of the lower West Side. Homeless, they have a hundred homes. They flit from furnished room to furnished room, transients forever—transients in abode, transients in heart and mind. They sing "Home, Sweet Home" in ragtime; they carry their lares et penates in a bandbox; their vine is entwined about a picture hat; a rubber plant is their fig tree.

Hence the houses of this district, having had a thousand dwellers, should have a thousand tales to tell, mostly dull ones, no doubt; but it would be strange if there could not be found a ghost or two in the wake of all these vagrant guests.

One evening after dark, a young man prowled among these crumbling red mansions, ringing their bells. At the twelfth he rested his lean hand-baggage upon the step and wiped the dust from his hatband and forehead. The bell sounded faint and far away in some remote, hollow depths.

To the door of this, the twelfth house whose bell he had rung, came a housekeeper who made him think of an unwholesome, surfeited worm that had eaten its nut to a hollow shell and now sought to fill the vacancy with edible lodgers.

He asked if there was a room to let.

"Come in," said the housekeeper. Her voice came from her throat; her throat seemed lined with fur. "I have the third-floor-back, vacant since a week back. Should you wish to look at it?"

The young man followed her up the stairs.

"This is the room," said the housekeeper, from her furry throat. "It's a nice room. It ain't often vacant. I had some most elegant people in it last summer—no trouble at all, and paid in advance to the minute. Sprowls and Mooney kept it three months. They done a vaudeville sketch. Miss B'retta Sprowls—you may have heard of her—Oh, that was just the stage names—right there over the dresser is where the marriage certificate hung, framed. It's a room everybody likes. It never stays idle long."

"Do you have many theatrical people rooming here?" asked the young man.

"They comes and goes. A good proportion of my lodgers is connected with the theatres. Yes, sir, this is the theatrical district. Actor people never stays long anywhere. I get my share. Yes, they comes and they goes."

He engaged the room, paying for a week in advance. He was tired, he said, and would like to take possession at once. The room had been made ready, she said, even to towels and water. As the housekeeper moved away he put, for the thousandth time, the question that he carried at the end of his tongue.

"A young girl—Miss Vashner—Miss Eloise Vashner— do you remember such a one among your lodgers? She would be singing on the stage, most likely. A fair girl, of medium height and slender, with reddish gold hair and dark mole near her left eyebrow."

"No, I don't remember the name. Them stage people has names they change as often as their rooms. They comes and they goes. No, I don't call that one to mind."

No. Always no. Five months of ceaseless interrogation and the inevitable negative. So much time spent by day in questioning managers, agents, schools and choruses; by night among the audiences of theaters from all-star casts down to music halls so low that he dreaded to find what he most hoped for. He who had loved her best had tried to find her. He was sure that since her disappearance from home, this great, water-girt city held her somewhere, but it was like a monstrous quicksand, shifting its particles constantly, with no foundation, its upper granules of today buried tomorrow in ooze and slime.

The guest reclined, inert, upon a chair, while the room, confused in speech as though it were an apartment in Babel, tried to discourse to him of its diverse tenantry.

One by one, as the characters of a cryptograph become explicit, the little signs left by the furnished room's procession of guests developed a significance. The tiny fingerprints on the wall spoke of the little prisoners trying to feel their way to sun and air. A splattered stain, raying like the shadow of a bursting bomb, witnessed where a hurled glass or bottle had splintered with its contents against the wall. Across the pier glass had been scrawled, with a diamond ring in staggering letters, the name "Marie." It seemed that the succession of dwellers in the furnished room had turned in fury—perhaps tempted beyond forbearance by its garish coldness—and wreaked upon it their passions. It seemed incredible that all this malice and injury had been wrought upon the room by those who had called it for a time their home; and yet it may have been the cheated home instinct surviving blindly, the resenting rage at false household gods that had kindled their wrath. A hut that is our own we can sweep and adorn and cherish.

The young tenant in the chair allowed these thoughts to file, soft-shod, through his mind, while there drifted into the room furnished sounds and furnished scents.

Then suddenly, as he rested there, the room was filled with the strong, sweet odour of mignonette. It came as upon a single buffet of wind with such sureness and fragrance and emphasis that it almost seemed a living visitant. And the man cried aloud, "What dear?" as if he had been called, and sprang up and faced about. The rich odour clung to him and wrapped him around. He reached out his arms for it, all his senses for the time confused and commingled. How could one be peremptorily called by an odour? Surely it must have been a sound. But, was it not the sound that had touched, that had caressed him?

11

"She has been in this room," he cried, and he sprang to wrest from it a token, for he knew he would recognize the smallest thing that had belonged to her or that she had touched. This enveloping scent of mignonette, the odour that she had loved and made her own—whence came it?

The room had been but carelessly set in order. Scattered upon the flimsy dresser scarf were half a dozen hairpins. These he ignored, conscious of their triumphant lack of identity. Ransacking the drawers of the dresser he came upon a discarded, tiny, ragged handkerchief. He pressed it to his face. It was racy and insolent with heliotrope; he hurled it to the floor. In another drawer he found odd buttons, a theater program, a pawnbroker's card, two lost marshmallows, a book on the divination of dreams. In the last was a woman's black satin hair bow, which halted him, poised between ice and fire. But a black satin hair bow is an impersonal common ornament and tells no tales.

And then he traversed the room like a hound on the scent, skimming the walls, considering the corners of the bulging matting on his hands and knees, rummaging mantel and tables, the curtains and hangings, the drunken cabinet in the corner, for a visible sign, unable to perceive that she was there beside, around, against, within, above him, clinging to him, wooing him, calling him so poignantly through the finer senses that even his grosser ones became cognizant of the call. Once again he answered loudly, "Yes, dear!" and turned, wild-eyed, to gaze on vacancy, for he could not yet discern form and colour and love and outstretched arms in the odour of mignonette. Oh, God! whence that odour, and since when have odours had a voice to call? Thus he groped.

He sifted the room from end to end. He found dreary and

ignoble small records of many a peripatetic tenant; but of her whom he sought, and who may have lodged there, and whose spirit seemed to hover there, he found no trace.

And then he thought of the housekeeper.

He ran from the haunted room downstairs and to a door that showed a crack of light. She came out to his knock. He smothered his excitement as best he could.

"Will you tell me, madam," he besought her, "who occupied the room I have before I came?"

"Yes, sir. I can tell you again. 'Twas Sprowls and Mooney, as I said. Miss B'retta Sprowls it was in the theaters, but Missis Mooney she was. My house is well known for respectability. The marriage certificate hung, framed, on a nail over—"

"What kind of a lady was Miss Sprowls—in looks, I mean?"

"Why, black-haired, sir, short, and stout, with a comical face. They left a week ago Tuesday."

"And before they occupied it?"

"Why, there was a single gentleman connected with the draying business. He left owing me a week. Before him was Missis Crowder and her two children, that stayed four months; and back of them was old Mr. Doyle, whose sons paid for him. He kept the room for six months. That goes back a year, sir, and further I do not remember."

He thanked her and crept back to his room. The room was dead. The essence that had vivified it was gone. The perfume of mignonette had departed. In its place was the old, stale odour of mouldy house furniture, of atmosphere in storage.

The ebbing of his hope drained his faith. He sat staring at the yellow, singing gaslight. He turned out the light, turned the gas full on again and laid himself gratefully upon the bed.

∽

It was Mrs. McCool's night to go with the can for beer. So she fetched it and sat with Mrs. Purdy in one of those subterranean retreats where housekeepers foregather and the worm dieth seldom.

"I rented out my third-floor-back this evening," said Mrs. Purdy, across a fine circle of foam. "A young man took it. He went up to bed two hours ago."

"Now, did ye, Missis Purdy, ma'am?" said Mrs. McCool, with intense admiration. "You do be a wonder for rentin' rooms of that kind. And did ye tell him, then?" she concluded in a husky whisper laden with mystery.

"Rooms," said Mrs. Purdy, in her furriest tones, "are furnished for to rent. I did not tell him, Missis McCool."

"'Tis right ye are, ma'am; 'tis by renting rooms we kape alive. Ye have the rare sense for business, ma'am. There be many people will reject the rentin' of a room if they be told a suicide has been after dyin' in the bed of it."

"As you say, we has our living to be making," remarked Mrs. Purdy.

"Yis, ma'am; 'tis true. 'Tis just one wake ago this day I helped ye lay out the third-floor-back. A pretty slip of a colleen she was to be killin' herself wid the gas—a sweet little face she had, Missis Purdy, ma'am."

"She'd a-been called handsome, as you say," said Mrs. Purdy, assenting but critical, "but for that mole she had a-growin' by her left eyebrow. Do fill up your glass again, Missis McCool."

THE JUDGE'S HOUSE

by Bram Stoker

Born in Dublin in 1847, BRAM STOKER was such a sickly child that he was not expected to live past his first month, let alone live to produce a legendary work such as the gruesome tale of terror Dracula. But his mother, a champion of equal rights for women, instilled her drive for success in her young son, who not only overcame his weak health, but later won an award as an athletics champion at Trinity College.

As Stoker's stamina grew, so did his desire to learn. Soon he became an accomplished scholar, and when Walt Whitman's Leaves of Grass was first published, Stoker was one of the few who ardently supported it. This acute artistic sense led him to a job as a theater critic, and then as an editor for the Halfpenny Press in 1873.

It was sometime after his marriage to Florence Balcombe in 1878 that Stoker's writing career really took off. One night he had a horrifying vision in his sleep that later transformed itself into the story of Dracula, which eventually became an unforgettable nightmare for millions.

Now, here to trouble your sleep, is "The Judge's House," an eerie tale that sets a tone of mystery and dread when a weary college student secludes himself in the deserted house of a long-dead justice of the peace who has a penchant for inflicting pain. At the end, the young man sleeps soundly . . . but will you?

Whidth the time for his examination drew near, Malcolm Malcolmson made up his mind to go somewhere to read by himself. He packed a portmanteau with some clothes and all the books he required, and then took ticket for the first name on the local timetable which he did not know.

When at the end of three hours' journey he alighted at Benchurch, he felt satisfied that he had so far obliterated his tracks as to be sure of having a peaceful opportunity of pursuing his studies. He went straight to the one inn which the sleepy little place contained, and put up for the night. Malcolmson looked around the day after his arrival to try to find quarters more isolated than even so quiet an inn as "The Good Traveller" afforded. There was only one place which took his fancy, and it certainly satisfied his wildest ideas regarding quiet; in fact, quiet was not the proper word to apply to it—desolation was the only term conveying any suitable idea of its isolation. It was an old rambling, heavy-built house of the Jacobean style, with heavy gables and windows, unusually small, and set higher than was customary in such houses, and was surrounded with a high brick wall, massively built. Indeed, on examination, it looked more like a fortified house than an ordinary dwelling. But all these things pleased Malcolmson. His joy was increased when he realized beyond doubt that it was not at present inhabited.

From the post office he got the name of the agent, who was rarely surprised at the application to rent a part of the old house. Mr. Carnford, the local lawyer and agent, was a genial old gentleman, and frankly confessed his delight at anyone being willing to live in the house. "To tell you the truth," said he, "I should be only too happy, on behalf of the owners, to let anyone have the house rent free for a term of years if only to accustom the people here to see it inhabited. It has been so long empty that some kind of absurd prejudice has grown up about it, and this can be best put down by its occupation—if only," he added with a sly glance at Malcolmson, "by a scholar like yourself, who wants it quiet for a time."

Malcolmson thought it needless to ask the agent about the "absurd prejudice"; he knew he would get more information, if he should require it, on that subject from other quarters. He paid his three months' rent, got a receipt, and the name of an old woman who would probably undertake to "do" for him, and came away with the keys in his pocket. He then went to the landlady of the inn, who was a cheerful and most kindly person, and asked her advice as to such stores and provisions as he would be likely to require. She threw up her hands in amazement when he told her where he was going to settle himself.

"Not in the Judge's House!" she said, and grew pale as she spoke. He explained the locality of the house, saying that he did not know its name.

When he had finished she answered, "It is the Judge's House sure enough." He asked her to tell him about the place. She told him that it was so called locally because it had been many years before—how long she could not say, as she was herself from another part of the country, but she thought it must have been a hundred years or more—the abode of a judge who was held in great terror on account of his harsh sentences and his hostility to prisoners at Assizes. As to what there was against the house itself she could not tell. She had often asked, but no one could inform her; but there was a general feeling that there was *something*, and for her own part she would not take all the money in Drinkwater's Bank and

18

stay in the house an hour by herself. Then she apologized to Malcolmson for her disturbing talk.

"It is too bad of me, sir, and you—and a young gentle-man, too—if you will pardon me saying it, going to live there all alone. If you were my boy you wouldn't sleep there a night, not if I had to go there myself and pull the big alarm bell that's on the roof!" The good creature was so manifestly in earnest, and was so kindly in her intentions, that Malcolmson, although amused, was touched.

He told her kindly how much he appreciated her interest in him, and added, "But, my dear Mrs. Witham, indeed you need not be concerned about me! A man who is reading for the Mathematical Tripos has too much to think of to be dis-turbed by any of these mysterious 'somethings,' and his work is of too exact and prosaic a kind to allow of his having any corner in his mind for mysteries of any kind. Harmonical Progression, Permutations and Combinations, and Elliptic Functions have sufficient mysteries for me!" Mrs. Witham kindly undertook to see after his commissions, and he went himself to look for the old woman who had been recom-mended to him.

When he returned to the Judge's House with her, after an interval of a couple of hours, he found Mrs. Witham her-self waiting with several men and boys carrying parcels, and an upholsterer's man with a bed in a cart. She was evidently curious to see the inside of the house; and though manifestly so afraid of the "somethings" that at the slightest sound she clutched on to Malcolmson, whom she never left for a moment, went over the whole place.

After his examination of the house, Malcolmson decided to take up his abode in the great dining room; and Mrs.

Witham, with the aid of the charwoman, Mrs. Dempster, proceeded to arrange matters. When the hampers were brought in and unpacked, Malcolmson saw that with much kind forethought she had sent from her own kitchen sufficient provisions to last for a few days. Before going she expressed all sorts of kind wishes; and at the door turned and said, "And perhaps, sir, as the room is big and draughty it might be well to have one of those big screens put round your bed at night—though, truth to tell, I would die myself if I were to be so shut in with all kinds of—of· 'things,' that put their heads round the sides, or over the top, and look on me!" The image which she had called up was too much for her nerves, and she fled incontinently.

Mrs. Dempster sniffed in a superior manner as the landlady disappeared, and remarked that for her own part she wasn't afraid of all the bogies in the kingdom. "I'll tell you what it is, sir," she said, "bogies is all kinds and sorts of things—except bogies! Rats and mice, and beetles; and creaky doors, and loose slates, and broken panes. Look at the wainscot of the room! It is old—hundreds of years old! Do you think there's no rats and beetles there! And do you imagine, sir, that you won't see none of them! Rats is bogies, I tell you, and bogies is rats; and don't you get to think anything else!" She set to work with her cleaning; and by nightfall, when Malcolmson returned from his walk he found the room swept and tidied, a fire burning in the old hearth, the lamp lit, and the table spread for supper with Mrs. Witham's excellent fare. "This is comfort, indeed," he said, as he rubbed his hands.

When he had finished his supper, he got out his books again, put fresh wood on the fire, trimmed his lamp, and set himself down to a spell of real hard work. He went on with-

out a pause till about eleven o'clock, when he knocked off for
a bit to fix his fire and lamp, and to make himself a cup of tea.
He had always been a tea drinker, and during his college life
had sat late at work and had taken tea late. The rest was a
great luxury to him, and he enjoyed it with a sense of deli-
cious, voluptuous ease. As he sipped his hot tea he revelled
in the sense of isolation from his kind. Then it was that
he began to notice for the first time what a noise the rats
were making.

"Surely," he thought, "they cannot have been at it all the
time I was reading. Had they been, I must have noticed it!"
Presently, when the noise increased, he satisfied himself that
it was really new. It was evident that at first the rats had been
frightened at the presence of a stranger, and the light of fire
and lamp; but that as the time went on they had grown
bolder and were now disporting themselves as was their wont.

How busy they were! and hark to the strange noises! Up
and down behind the old wainscot, over the ceiling and under
the floor they raced, and gnawed, and scratched! Malcolmson
smiled to himself as he recalled to mind the saying of Mrs.
Dempster, "Bogies is rats, and rats is bogies!" The tea began
to have its effect of intellectual and nervous stimulus; he saw
with joy another long spell of work to be done before the
night was past, and in the sense of security which it gave him,
he allowed himself the luxury of a good look round the room.
He took his lamp in one hand, and went all around, wondering that so quaint and beautiful an old house had been so
long neglected. There were some old pictures on the walls,
but they were coated so thick with dust and dirt that he could
not distinguish any detail of them, though he held his lamp as
high as he could over his head. Here and there as he went

round, he saw some crack or hole blocked for a moment by the face of a rat with its bright eyes glittering in the light, but in an instant it was gone, and a squeak and a scamper followed.

The thing that most struck him, however, was the rope of the great alarm bell on the roof, which hung down in a corner of the room on the right-hand side of the fireplace. He pulled up close to the hearth a great high-backed carved oak chair, and sat down to his last cup of tea. When this was done he made up the fire, and went back to his work sitting at the corner of the table, having the fire to his left. For a while the rats disturbed him somewhat with their perpetual scampering, but he got accustomed to the noise, and he became so immersed in his work that everything in the world, except the problem which he was trying to solve, passed away from him.

He suddenly looked up, his problem was still unsolved, and there was in the air that sense of the hour before dawn, which is so dread to doubtful life. The noise of the rats had ceased. Indeed it seemed to him that it must have ceased but lately and that it was the sudden cessation which had disturbed him. As he looked, he started in spite of his *sang froid*.

There on the great high-backed carved oak chair by the right side of the fireplace sat an enormous rat, steadily glaring at him with baleful eyes. He made a motion to it as though to hunt it away, but it did not stir. Then he made the motion of throwing something. Still it did not stir, but showed its great white teeth angrily, and its cruel eyes shone in the lamplight with an added vindictiveness.

Malcolmson felt amazed, and seizing the poker from the hearth ran at it to kill it. Before, however, he could strike it, the rat, with a squeak that sounded like the concentration of hate, jumped upon the floor, and, running up the rope of

the alarm bell, disappeared in the darkness. Instantly, strange to say, the noisy scampering of the rats in the wainscot began again.

By this time Malcolmson's mind was quite off the problem; and as a shrill cock-crow outside told him of the approach of morning, he went to bed and to sleep.

He slept so sound that he was not even waked by Mrs. Dempster coming in to make up his room. It was only when she had tidied up the place and got his breakfast ready and tapped on the screen which closed in his bed that he woke. He was a little tired still after his night's hard work, but a strong cup of tea soon freshened him up, and, taking his book, he went out for his morning walk. On his return he looked in to see Mrs. Witham and to thank her for her kindness. When she saw him coming through the bay window of her sanctum, she came out to meet him and asked him in.

She looked at him searchingly and shook her head as she said, "You must not overdo it, sir. You are paler this morning than you should be. Too late hours and too hard work on the brain isn't good for any man! But tell me, sir, how did you pass the night? But, my heart! sir, I was glad when Mrs. Dempster told me this morning that you were all right and sleeping sound when she went in."

"Oh, I was all right," he answered, smiling, "the 'somethings' didn't worry me, as yet. Only the rats; and they had a circus, I tell you, all over the place. There was one wicked looking old devil that sat up on my own chair by the fire, and wouldn't go till I took the poker to him, and then he ran up the rope of the alarm bell and got to somewhere up the wall or the ceiling—I couldn't see where, it was so dark."

"Mercy on us," said Mrs. Witham, "an old devil, and

sitting on a chair by the fireside! Take care, sir! take care! There's many a true word spoken in jest."

"How do you mean? 'Pon my word I don't understand."

"An old devil! The old devil, perhaps. There! sir, you needn't laugh," for Malcolmson had broken into a hearty peal. "You young folks thinks it easy to laugh at things that makes older ones shudder. Never mind, sir! never mind! Please God, you'll laugh all the time. It's what I wish you myself!" and the good lady beamed all over in sympathy with his enjoyment, her fears gone for a moment.

"Oh, forgive me!" said Malcolmson presently. "Don't think me rude; but the idea was too much for me—that the old devil himself was on the chair last night!" And at the thought he laughed again. Then he went home to dinner.

This evening the scampering of the rats began earlier; indeed it had been going on before his arrival, and only ceased whilst his presence, by its freshness, disturbed them. After dinner he began to work as before. Tonight the rats disturbed him more than they had done on the previous night. Now and again as they disturbed him Malcolmson made a sound to frighten them, smiting the table with his hand or giving a fierce "Hsh, hsh," so that they fled straightway to their holes.

And so the early part of the night wore on; and despite the noise Malcolmson got more and more immersed in his work.

All at once he stopped, as on the previous night, being overcome by a sudden sense of silence. There was not the faintest sound of gnaw, or scratch, or squeak. The silence was as of the grave. He remembered the odd occurrence of the previous night, and instinctively he looked at the chair standing close by the fireside. And then a very odd sensation thrilled through him.

There, on the great old high-backed carved oak chair beside the fireplace sat the same enormous rat, steadily glaring at him with baleful eyes.

Instinctively he took the nearest thing to his hand, a book of logarithms, and flung it at it. The book was badly aimed and the rat did not stir, so again the poker performance of the previous night was repeated; and again the rat, being closely pursued, fled up the rope of the alarm bell.

Strangely too, the departure of this rat was instantly followed by the renewal of the noise made by the general rat community. On this occasion, as on the previous one, Malcolmson could not see at what part of the room the rat disappeared, for the green shade of his lamp left the upper part of the room in darkness, and the fire had burned low.

On looking at his watch he found it was close on midnight; and he made up his fire and made himself his nightly pot of tea. He had got through a good spell of work, and thought himself entitled to a cigarette; so he sat on the great carved oak chair before the fire and enjoyed it. Whilst smoking he began to think that he would like to know where the rat disappeared to, for he had certain ideas for the morrow not entirely disconnected with a rat trap. Accordingly he lit another lamp and placed it so that it would shine well into the right-hand corner of the wall by the fireplace. Then he got all the books he had with him, and placed them handy to throw at the vermin. Finally he lifted the rope of the alarm bell and placed the end of it on the table, fixing the extreme end under the lamp. As he handled it he could not help noticing how pliable it was, especially for so strong a rope, and one not in use. "You could hang a man with it," he thought to himself.

When his preparations were made he looked around, and

said complacently, "There now, my friend, I think we shall learn something of you this time!" He began his work again, and though as before somewhat disturbed at first by the noise of the rats, soon lost himself in his propositions and problems.

Again he was called to his immediate surroundings suddenly. This time it might not have been the sudden silence only which took his attention; there was a slight movement of the rope, and the lamp moved. Without stirring, he looked to see if his pile of books was within range, and then cast his eye along the rope. As he looked he saw the great rat drop from the rope on the oak armchair and sit there glaring at him. He raised a book in his right hand, and taking careful aim, flung it at the rat. The latter, with a quick movement, sprang aside and dodged the missile. He then took another book, and a third, and flung them one after another at the rat, but each time unsuccessfully. At last, as he stood with a book poised in his hand to throw, the rat squeaked and seemed to be afraid. This made Malcolmson more than ever eager to strike, and the book flew and struck the rat a resounding blow. It gave a terrified squeak, and turning on its pursuer a look of terrible malevolence, ran up the chairback and made a great jump to the rope of the alarm bell and ran up it like lightning. The lamp rocked under the sudden strain, but it was a heavy one and did not topple over. Malcolmson kept his eyes on the rat, and saw it by the light of the second lamp leap to a molding of the wainscot and disappear through a hole in one of the great pictures which hung on the wall, obscured and invisible through its coating of dirt and dust.

"I shall look up my friend's habitation in the morning," said the student, as he went over to collect his books. "The third picture from the fireplace; I shall not forget." He picked up the books one by one, commenting on them as he lifted them. "*Conic Sections* he does not mind, nor *Cycloidal Oscillations*, nor the *Principia*, nor *Quaternions*, nor *Thermodynamics*. Now for the book that fetched him!"

Malcolmson took it up and looked at it. As he did so he started, and a sudden pallor overspread his face. He looked round uneasily and shivered slightly, as he murmured to himself, "The Bible my mother gave me! What an odd coincidence." He sat down to work again, and the rats in the wainscot renewed their gambols. They did not disturb him, however; somehow their presence gave him a sense of companionship. But he could not attend to his work, and after striving to master the subject on which he was engaged, gave it up in despair, and went to bed as the first streak of dawn stole in through the eastern window.

He slept heavily but uneasily, and dreamed much; and when Mrs. Dempster woke him late in the morning he seemed ill at ease, and for a few minutes did not seem to realize exactly where he was. His first request rather surprised the servant.

"Mrs. Dempster, when I am out today, I wish you would get the steps and dust or wash those pictures—specially that one, the third from the fireplace—I want to see what they are."

Late in the afternoon Malcolmson worked at his books in the shaded walk, and the cheerfulness of the previous day came back to him as the day wore on, and he found that his reading was progressing well. He had worked out to a satisfactory conclusion all the problems which had as yet baffled him, and it was in a state of jubilation that he paid a visit to Mrs. Witham at "The Good Traveller." He found a stranger in the cozy sitting-room with the landlady, who was introduced to him as Dr. Thornhill. She was not quite at ease, and this, combined with the Doctor's plunging at once into a series of questions, made Malcolmson come to the conclusion that his presence was not an accident. So without preliminary he said, "Dr. Thornhill, I shall with pleasure answer you any question you may choose to ask me if you will answer me one question first."

The Doctor seemed surprised, but he smiled and answered at once. "Done! What is it?"

"Did Mrs. Witham ask you to come here and advise me?"

Dr. Thornhill for a moment was taken aback, and Mrs. Witham got fiery red and turned away; but the Doctor was a frank and ready man, and he answered at once and openly. "She did, but she didn't intend you to know it. She told me that she did not like the idea of your being in that house all by yourself, and that she thought you took too much strong tea. In fact, she wants me to advise you, if possible, to give up the tea and the very late hours. I was a keen student in my time, so I suppose I may take the liberty of a college man, and without offense, advise you not quite as a stranger."

Malcolmson with a smile held out his hand. "Shake! as they say in America," he said. "I must thank you for your kindness and Mrs. Witham too, and your kindness deserves a return on my part. I promise to take no more strong tea—no tea at all till you let me—and I shall go to bed tonight at one o'clock at latest. Will that do?"

"Capital," said the Doctor. "Now tell us all that you noticed in the old house," and so Malcolmson, then and there, told in minute detail all that had happened in the last two nights. He was interrupted every now and then by some exclamation from Mrs. Witham, till finally when he told of the episode of the Bible the landlady's pent-up emotions found vent in a shriek; and it was not till a stiff glass of brandy and water had been administered that she grew composed again.

Dr. Thornhill listened with a face of growing gravity, and when the narrative was complete and Mrs. Witham had been restored he asked, "The rat always went up the rope of the alarm bell?"

"Always."

"I suppose you know," said the Doctor after a pause, "what the rope is?"

"No!"

"It is," said the Doctor slowly, "the very rope which the hangman used for all the victims of the Judge's judicial rancor!" Here he was interrupted by another scream from Mrs. Witham, and steps had to be taken for her recovery. Malcolmson having looked at his watch, and found that it was close to his dinner hour, had gone home before her complete recovery.

When Mrs. Witham was herself again she almost assailed the Doctor with angry questions as to what he meant by putting such horrible ideas into the poor young man's mind.

Dr. Thornhill replied, "My dear madam, I had a distinct purpose in it! I wanted to draw his attention to the bell rope, and to fix it there. It may be that he is in a highly overwrought state, and has been studying too much, although I am bound to say that he seems as sound and healthy a young man, mentally and bodily, as ever I saw—but then the rats—and that suggestion of the devil." The doctor shook his head and went on. "I would have offered to go and stay the first night with him but that I felt sure it would have been a cause of offense. He may get in the night some strange fright or hallucination; and if he does, I want him to pull that rope. All alone as he is it will give us warning, and we may reach him in time to be of service. Do not be alarmed if Benchurch gets a surprise before morning."

"Oh, Doctor, what do you mean? What do you mean?"

"I mean this; that possibly—nay, more probably—we shall hear the great alarm bell from the Judge's House tonight," and the Doctor made about as effective an exit as could be thought of.

When Malcolmson arrived home he found that it was a little after his usual time, and Mrs. Dempster had gone away. For a few minutes after his entrance the noise of the rats ceased; but so soon as they became accustomed to his presence they began again. He was glad to hear them, for he felt once more the feeling of companionship in their noise, and his mind ran back to the strange fact that they only ceased to manifest themselves when that other—the great rat with the baleful eyes—came upon the scene. The reading lamp only was lit, and its green shade kept the ceiling and the upper part of the room in darkness, so that the cheerful light from the hearth, spreading over the floor and shining on the white cloth laid over the end of the table, was warm and cheery. Malcolmson sat down to his dinner with a good appetite and a buoyant spirit. After his dinner and a cigarette he sat steadily down to work, determined not to let anything disturb him.

For an hour or so he worked all right, and then his thoughts began to wander from his books. The actual circumstances around him, the calls on his physical attention, and his nervous susceptibility were not to be denied. By this time the wind had become a gale, and the gale a storm. Even the great alarm bell on the roof must have felt the force of the wind, for the rope rose and fell slightly, as though the bell were moved a little from time to time, and the limber rope fell on the oak floor with a hard and hollow sound.

As Malcolmson listened to it he bethought himself of the doctor's words, "It is the rope which the hangman used for the victims of the Judge's judicial rancour," and he went over to the corner of the fireplace and took it in his hand to look at it. There seemed a sort of deadly interest in it, and as he stood there he lost himself for a moment in speculation as to who these victims were, and the grim wish of the Judge to have such a ghastly relic ever under his eyes. As he stood there the swaying of the bell on the roof still lifted the rope now and again; but presently there came a new sensation—a sort of tremor in the rope, as though something was moving along it.

Looking up instinctively Malcolmson saw the great rat coming slowly down towards him, glaring at him steadily. He dropped the rope and started back with a muttered curse, and the rat turning ran up the rope again and disappeared, and at the same instant, Malcolmson became conscious that the noise of the rats, which had ceased for a while, began again.

All this set him thinking, and it occurred to him that he had not investigated the lair of the rat or looked at the pictures, as he had intended. He lit the other lamp, and, holding it up, went and stood opposite the third picture from the fireplace on the right-hand side where he had seen the rat disappear on the previous night.

At the first glance he started back so suddenly that he almost dropped the lamp, and a deadly pallor overspread his face. But he was young and plucky, and pulled himself together, and after the pause of a few seconds stepped forward again, raised the lamp, and examined the picture which had been dusted and washed, and now stood out clearly.

It was of a judge dressed in his robes of scarlet and ermine. His face was strong and merciless, evil, crafty, and vindictive, with a sensual mouth, hooked nose of ruddy colour, and shaped like the beak of a bird of prey. The eyes were of peculiar brilliance and with a terribly malignant expression. As he looked at them, Malcolmson grew cold, for he saw there the very counterpart of the eyes of the great rat. The lamp almost fell from his hand, he saw the rat with its baleful eyes peering out through the hole in the corner of the picture, and noted the sudden cessation of the noise of the other rats. However, he pulled himself together, and went on with his examination of the picture.

The Judge was seated in a great high-backed carved oak chair, on the right-hand side of a great stone fireplace where, in the corner, a rope hung down from the ceiling, its end lying coiled on the floor. With a feeling of something like horror, Malcolmson recognized the scene of the room as it stood, and gazed around in an awe struck manner as though he expected to find some strange presence behind him. Then he looked over to the corner of the fireplace—and with a loud cry he let the lamp fall from his hand.

There, in the Judge's armchair, with the rope hanging behind, sat the rat with the Judge's baleful eyes, now intensi-fied and with a fiendish leer. Save for the howling of the storm without there was silence.

The fallen lamp recalled Malcolmson to himself. Fortunately it was of metal, and so the oil was not spilt.

However, the practical need of attending to it settled at once his nervous apprehensions. When he had turned it out, he wiped his brow and thought for a moment.

"This will not do," he said to himself. "If I go on like this I shall become a crazy fool. This must stop! I promised the Doctor I would not take tea. Faith, he was pretty right! My nerves must have been getting into a queer state. Funny I did not notice it. I never felt better in my life. However, it is all right now, and I shall not be such a fool again." Then he mixed himself a good stiff glass of brandy and water and resolutely sat down to his work.

It was nearly an hour when he looked up from his book, disturbed by the sudden stillness. Malcolmson listened attentively, and presently heard a thin, squeaking noise, very faint. It came from the corner of the room where the rope hung down, and he thought it was the creaking of the rope on the floor as the swaying of the bell raised and lowered it. Looking up, however, he saw in the dim light the great rat clinging to the rope and gnawing it. The rope was already nearly gnawed through—he could see the lighter colour where the strands were laid bare. As he looked the job was completed, and the severed end of the rope fell clattering on the oaken floor, whilst for an instant the great rat remained like a knob or tassel at the end of the rope, which now began to sway to and fro. Malcolmson felt for a moment another pang of terror as he thought that now the possibility of calling the outer world to his assistance was cut off, but an intense anger took its place, and seizing the book he was reading he hurled it at the rat. The blow was well aimed, but before the missile could reach it the rat dropped off and struck the floor with a soft thud. Malcolmson instantly rushed over towards it, but it darted away and disappeared in the darkness of the shadows of the room. Malcolmson felt that his work was over for the night, and determined then and there to vary the monotony of the proceedings by a hunt for the rat. From where he stood, Malcolmson saw right opposite to him the third picture on the wall from the right of the fireplace. He rubbed his eyes in surprise, and then a great fear began to come upon him.

In the center of the picture was a great irregular patch of brown canvas, as fresh as when it was stretched on the frame. The background was as before, with chair and chimney-corner and rope, but the figure of the Judge had disappeared.

Malcolmson, almost in a chill of horror, turned slowly round, and then he began to shake and tremble like a man in a palsy. His strength seemed to have left him, and he was incapable of action or movement, hardly even of thought. He could only see and hear.

There, on the great high-backed carved oak chair sat the Judge in his robes of scarlet and ermine, with his baleful eyes glaring vindictively, and a smile of triumph on the resolute, cruel mouth, as he lifted with his hands a *black cap*. Malcolmson felt as if the blood was running from his heart, as one does in moments of prolonged suspense. There was a singing in his ears. Without, he could hear the roar and howl of the tempest, and through it, swept on the storm, came the striking of midnight by the great chimes in the marketplace. He stood for a space of time that seemed to him endless, still as a statue and with wide-open, horror-struck eyes, breathless. As the clock struck, so the smile of triumph on the Judge's face intensified, and at the last stroke of midnight he placed the black cap on his head.

Slowly and deliberately the Judge rose from his chair and

picked up the piece of rope of the alarm bell which lay on the floor, drew it through his hands as if he enjoyed the touch, and then deliberately began to knot one end of it, fashioning it into a noose. Then he began to move along the table on the opposite side to Malcolmson, keeping his eyes on him until he had passed him, when with a quick movement he stood in front of the door. Malcolmson then began to feel that he was trapped, and tried to think of what he should do. There was some fascination in the Judge's eyes, which he never took off him, and he had, perforce, to look. He saw the Judge approach—still keeping between him and the door—and raise the noose and throw it towards him as if to entangle him. With a great effort he made a quick movement to one side, and saw the rope fall beside him, and heard it strike the oaken floor. Again the Judge raised the noose and tried to ensnare him, ever keeping his baleful eyes fixed on him, and each time by a mighty effort the student just managed to evade it. So this went on for many times, the Judge seeming never discouraged nor discomposed at failure, but playing as a cat does with a mouse. At last, in despair which had reached its climax, Malcolmson cast a quick glance round him. The lamp seemed to have blazed up, and there was a fairly good light in the room. At the many rat-holes and in the chinks and crannies of the wainscot he saw the rats' eyes; and this aspect, that was purely physical, gave him a gleam of comfort. He looked around and saw that the rope of the great alarm bell was laden with rats. Every inch of it was covered with them, and more and more were pouring through the small circular hole in the ceiling whence it emerged, so that with their weight the bell was beginning to sway. Hark! it had swayed till the clapper had touched the bell. The sound was but a tiny one, but the bell was only beginning to sway, and it would increase.

At the sound the Judge, who had been keeping his eyes fixed on Malcolmson, looked up, and a scowl of diabolical anger overspread his face. A dreadful peal of thunder broke overhead as he raised the rope again, whilst the rats kept running up and down the rope as though working against time. This time, instead of throwing it, he drew close to his victim, and held open the noose as he approached. As he came closer there seemed something paralyzing in his very presence, and Malcolmson stood rigid as a corpse. He felt the Judge's icy fingers touch his throat as he adjusted the rope. Then the Judge, taking the rigid form of the student in his arms, carried him over and placed him standing in the oak chair, and stepping up beside him, put his hand up and caught the end of the swaying rope of the alarm bell. As he raised his hand the rats fled squeaking, and disappeared through the hole in the ceiling. Taking the end of the noose which was round Malcolmson's neck he tied it to the hanging bell-rope, and then descending, pulled away the chair.

When the alarm bell of the Judge's House began to sound a crowd soon assembled. They knocked loudly at the door, but there was no reply. Then they burst in the door, and poured into the great dining room, the Doctor at the head. There at the end of the rope of the great alarm bell hung the body of the student, and on the face of the Judge in the picture was a malignant smile.

THE LOST GHOST

by Mary E. Wilkins Freeman

Born on Halloween in 1852, MARY ELEANOR WILKINS FREEMAN *was too weak as a child to attend school. But fortunately for her readers, she overcame her frailty and lived to the age of seventy-seven, producing two-hundred and thirty-eight short stories, twelve novels, one play, and two volumes of poetry.*

She was first published under her maiden name of Wilkins with a book of verse entitled Decorative Placques *in 1883. For the next two decades she supported herself and an aunt with her writing. During that time she was also Oliver Wendell Holmes's secretary, and he introduced her to the famous Massachusetts writers of the time.*

In 1891 she made a name for herself with the short story "A New England Nun," and in 1902 she married Dr. Charles Manning Freeman. The two had no children and lived in Metuchen, New Jersey, until she died on March 13th, 1930.

Freeman often described New England villages in her work and the frustrated lives of the people who inhabited them. In "The Lost Ghost," one such villager, Mrs. Meserve, is reserved at first about telling her friend her most unusual supernatural experience. But, to add a little spice to an otherwise dull afternoon, she shares the following eerie tale about a neglected little ghost connected to her own shocking past.

Mrs. John Emerson, sitting with her needlework beside the window, looked out and saw Mrs. Rhoda Meserve coming down the street. She knew by a certain something about her general carriage—a thrusting forward of the neck, a bustling hitch of the shoulders—that she had important news.

Mrs. Meserve was a pretty woman; her clear-cut, nervous face, as delicately tinted as a shell, looked brightly from the plumy brim of a black hat at Mrs. Emerson in the window. Mrs. Emerson was glad to see her coming. She returned the greeting with enthusiasm.

"Good afternoon," said she. "I declare, I'm real glad to see you. I've been alone all day. I thought of coming over to your house this afternoon, but I couldn't bring my sewing very well. I am putting the ruffles on my new black dress skirt."

"Well, I didn't have a thing on hand except my crochet work," responded Mrs. Meserve, "and I thought I'd just run over a few minutes."

"I'm real glad you did," repeated Mrs. Emerson.

Mrs. Meserve settled herself in the parlor rocking chair, while Mrs. Emerson carried her shawl and hat into the little adjoining bedroom. When she returned Mrs. Meserve was rocking peacefully and was already at work hooking blue wool in and out.

Mrs. Emerson waited for the news. Finally she could wait no longer. "Well, what's the news?" said she.

"Well, I don't know as there's anything very particular," hedged the other woman, prolonging the situation.

"Yes, there is; you can't cheat me," replied Mrs. Emerson.

"Now, how do you know?"

"By the way you look."

Mrs. Meserve laughed consciously and rather vainly. "Well, there is some news. Simon came home with it this noon. He heard it in South Dayton. The old Sergeant place is let."

Mrs. Emerson dropped her sewing and stared. "Who to?"

"Why, some folks from Boston that moved to South Dayton last year. They haven't been satisfied with the house they had there—it wasn't large enough. You know the old Sergeant house is a splendid place."

"Yes, it's the handsomest house in town, but—"

"Oh, Simon said they told him about that and he just laughed. Said he wasn't afraid and neither was his wife and sister. Said he'd risk ghosts rather than little tucked-up sleeping-rooms without any sun, like they've had in the Dayton house. Said he'd rather risk *seeing* ghosts, than risk being ghosts themselves."

"Oh, well," said Mrs. Emerson, "it is a beautiful house, and maybe there isn't anything in those stories. I never took much stock in them. All I thought was—if his wife was nervous."

"Nothing in creation would hire me to go into a house that I'd ever heard a word against of that kind," declared Mrs. Meserve with emphasis. "I wouldn't go into that house if they would give me the rent. I've seen enough of haunted houses to last me as long as I live."

Mrs. Emerson's face acquired the expression of a hunting hound. "Have you?" she asked in an intense whisper.

"Yes, I have. I don't want any more of it."

"Before you came here?"

"Yes, before I was married—when I was quite a girl."

"Did you really live in a house that was—" she whispered fearfully. "Did you really ever—see—anything—"

Mrs. Meserve nodded.

"You didn't see anything that did you any harm?"

"No, I didn't see anything that did me harm looking at it in one way, but it didn't do anybody in this world any good to see things that haven't any business to be seen in it. You never get over it."

There was a moment's silence. Mrs. Emerson's features seemed to sharpen. "Well, of course I don't want to urge you," said she, "if you don't feel like talking about it; but maybe it might do you good to tell it out, if it's on your mind, worrying you."

"I never told anybody but Simon," said Mrs. Meserve. "I never felt as if it was wise perhaps. I didn't know what folks might think. Simon advised me not to talk about it. He said lots of folks would sooner tell folks my head wasn't right than to own up they couldn't see through it."

"I'm sure I wouldn't say so," returned Mrs. Emerson reproachfully. "You know better than that, I hope."

"Yes, I do," replied Mrs. Meserve. "I know you wouldn't say so."

"And I wouldn't tell it to a soul if you didn't want me to."

"Well, I'd rather you wouldn't."

Mrs. Emerson took up her dress skirt again; Mrs. Meserve hooked up another loop of blue wool. Then she began:

"Of course," said she, "I ain't going to say positively that I believe or disbelieve in ghosts, but all I can tell you is what I saw. There hasn't been a day nor a night since it happened that I haven't thought of it, and always I have felt the shivers go down my back when I did."

"That's an awful feeling," Mrs. Emerson said.

"Ain't it? Well, it happened before I was married, when I was a girl and lived in East Wilmington. It was the first year

I lived there. I went there to teach school, and I went to board with a Mrs. Amelia Dennison and her sister, Mrs. Bird. Abby, her name was—Abby Bird. She was a widow; she had never had any children. She had a little money—Mrs. Dennison didn't have any—and she had come to East Wilmington and bought the house they lived in. It was a real pretty house, though it was very old and run down. It had cost Mrs. Bird a good deal to put it in order. I guess that was the reason they took me to board. I guess they thought it would help along a little.

"Anyhow, they took me to board, and I thought I was pretty lucky to get in there. I thought I hadn't been in such a nice place since I lost my own home, until I had been there about three weeks.

"I had been there about three weeks before I found it out, though I guess it had been going on ever since they had been in the house, and that was 'most four months. They hadn't said anything about it, and I didn't wonder, for there they had just bought the house and been to so much expense and trouble fixing it up.

"Well, I went there in September. I remember it was a real cold fall, there was a frost the middle of September, and I had to put on my winter coat. I remember when I came home that night, I took off my coat downstairs and laid it on the table in the front entry. Mrs. Bird called after me as I went upstairs that I ought not to leave it in the front entry for fear somebody might come in and take it, but I only laughed and called back to her that I wasn't afraid. I never was much afraid of burglars.

"Well, though it was hardly the middle of September, it was a real cold night. There was a fire in my little wood-stove.

Mrs. Bird made it, I know. She was a real motherly sort of woman; she always seemed to be the happiest when she was doing something to make other folks happy and comfortable.

"Well, that night I sat down beside my nice little fire and ate an apple. I was having a beautiful time, and thinking how lucky I was to have got board in such a place with such nice folks, when I heard a queer little sound at my door. For a minute I thought it was a mouse. But I waited and it came again, and then I made up my mind it was a knock, but a very little scared one, so I said, 'Come in.'

"But nobody came in, and then presently I heard the knock again. Then I got up and opened the door, thinking it was very queer, and I had a frightened feeling without knowing why.

"Well, I opened the door, and the first thing I noticed was a draught of cold air. Then I saw something. I saw my coat first. The thing that held it was so small that I couldn't see much of anything else. Then I saw a little white face with eyes so scared and wishful that they seemed as if they might eat a hole in anybody's heart. It was a dreadful little face, with something about it which made it different from any other face on earth, but it was so pitiful that somehow it did away a good deal with the dreadfulness. And there were two little hands spotted purple with the cold, holding up my winter coat, and a strange little far-away voice said: 'I can't find my mother.'

"'For Heaven's sake,' I said, 'who are you?'

"Then the little voice said again: 'I can't find my mother.'

"All the time I could smell the cold and I saw that it was about the child; that cold was clinging to her as if she had come out of some deadly cold place. Well, I took my coat, I did not know what else to do, and the cold was clinging to that. When I had the coat I could see the child more plainly. She was dressed in one little white garment made very simply. It was a nightgown, only very long, quite covering her feet, and I could see dimly through it her little thin body mottled purple with the cold. Her face did not look so cold; that was a clear waxen white. She would have been very beautiful if she had not been so dreadful.

"'Who are you?' says I again, looking at her.

"She looked at me with her terrible pleading eyes and did not say anything.

"'What are you?' says I. Then she went away. She did not seem to run or walk like other children. She flitted, like one of those little filmy white butterflies, that don't seem like real ones they are so light, and move as if they had no weight. But she looked back from the head of the stairs. 'I can't find my mother,' said she, and I never heard such a voice.

"'Who is your mother?' says I, but she was gone.

"Well, I thought for a moment I should faint away. The room got dark and I heard a singing in my ears. Then I flung my coat onto the bed. My hands were as cold as ice from holding it, and I stood in my door, and called first Mrs. Bird and then Mrs. Dennison. I thought I should never make any-body hear, but I could hear them stepping about downstairs, and I could smell biscuits baking for supper. Somehow the smell of those biscuits seemed the only natural thing left to keep me in my right mind. I didn't dare go over those stairs. I just stood there and called, and finally I heard the entry door open and Mrs. Bird called back.

"'What is it? Did you call, Miss Arms?'

"'Come up here; come up here as quick as you can, both

of you,' I screamed out; 'quick, quick, quick!'

"I heard Mrs. Bird tell Mrs. Dennison: 'Come quick, Amelia, something is the matter in Miss Arms' room.' It struck me as very queer, indeed, when they both got upstairs and I saw that they knew what had happened, or that they knew of what nature the happening was.

"'What is it, dear?' asked Mrs. Bird, and her pretty, loving voice had a strained sound. I saw her look at Mrs. Dennison and I saw Mrs. Dennison look back at her.

"'For God's sake,' says I, and I never spoke so before—'for God's sake, what was it brought my coat upstairs?'

"'What was it like?' asked Mrs. Dennison in a sort of failing voice, and she looked at her sister again and her sister looked back at her.

"'It was a child I have never seen here before. It looked like a child,' says I, 'but I never saw a child so dreadful, and it had on a nightgown, and said she couldn't find her mother. Who was it?'

"I thought for a minute Mrs. Dennison was going to faint, but Mrs. Bird hung onto her and rubbed her hands, and whispered in her ear (she had the cooingest kind of voice), and I ran and got her a glass of cold water. I tell you I didn't waste much time going down those stairs and out into the kitchen for a glass of water. I pumped as if the house was afire, and I grabbed the first thing I came across in the shape of a tumbler—it was a painted one that Mrs. Dennison's Sunday school class gave her, and it was meant for a flower vase.

"Well, I filled it and then ran upstairs. I felt every minute as if something would catch my feet, and I held the glass to Mrs. Dennison's lips, while Mrs. Bird held her head up, and she took a good long swallow.

"The water seemed to do Mrs. Dennison good, for presently she pushed Mrs. Bird away and sat up. She had been lying down on my bed. "'I'm all over it now,' says she, but she was terribly white, and her eyes looked as if they saw something outside things. Mrs. Bird wasn't much better, but she always had a sort of settled sweet, good look that nothing could disturb to any great extent. I knew I looked dreadful, for I caught a glimpse of myself in the glass, and I would hardly have known who it was.

"Mrs. Dennison, she slid off the bed and walked sort of tottery to a chair. 'I was silly to give way so,' says she.

"'No, you wasn't silly, sister,' says Mrs. Bird. 'I don't know what this means any more than you do, but whatever it is, no one ought to be called silly for being overcome by anything so different from other things which we have known all our lives.'

"Mrs. Dennison looked at her sister, then she looked at me, then back at her sister again, and Mrs. Bird spoke as if she had been asked a question.

"'Yes,' says she, 'I do think Miss Arms ought to be told— that is, I think she ought to be told all we know ourselves.'

"'That isn't much,' said Mrs. Dennison with a dying-away sort of sigh. She looked as if she might faint away again any minute. She was a real delicate-looking woman, but it turned out she was a good deal stronger than poor Mrs. Bird.

"'No, there isn't much we do know,' says Mrs. Bird, 'but what little there is she ought to know. I felt as if she ought to when she first came here.'

"'Well, I didn't feel quite right about it,' said Mrs. Dennison, 'but I kept hoping it might stop, and any way, that it might never trouble her, and you had put so much in the house, and we needed the money, and I didn't know but she might be nervous and think she couldn't come, and I didn't want to take a man boarder.'

"'And aside from the money, we were very anxious to have you come, my dear,' says Mrs. Bird.

"'Yes,' says Mrs. Dennison, 'we wanted the young company in the house; we were lonesome, and we both of us took a great liking to you the minute we set eyes on you.'

"And I guess they meant what they said, both of them. They were beautiful women, and nobody could be any kinder to me than they were, and I never blamed them for not telling me before, and, as they said, there really wasn't much to tell.

"They hadn't any sooner fairly bought the house, and moved into it, than they begin to see and hear things. Mrs. Bird said they were sitting together in the sitting-room one evening when they heard it the first time. She said her sister was knitting lace and she was reading the *Missionary Herald*, when all of a sudden they heard something. She heard it first and she laid down her *Missionary Herald* and listened, and then Mrs. Dennison saw her listening and she drops her lace. 'What is it you're listening to, Abby?' says she. Then it came again and they both heard, and the cold shivers went down their backs to hear it, though they didn't know why. 'It's the cat, isn't it?' says Mrs. Bird.

"'It isn't any cat,' says Mrs. Dennison.

"'Oh, I guess it *must* be the cat; maybe she's got a mouse,' says Mrs. Bird. Then she opens the door and calls, 'Kitty, kitty, kitty!'

"Well, she called 'Kitty, kitty, kitty!' and sure enough the kitty came, and when he came in the door he gave a big yowl that didn't sound unlike what they had heard.

"'There, sister, here he is; you see it was the cat,' says Mrs. Bird.

"But Mrs. Dennison she eyed the cat, and she give a great screech. 'Somethin's got hold of that cat's tail,' says Mrs. Dennison. 'Somethin's got hold of his tail. It's pulled straight out, an' he can't get away. Just hear him yowl!'

"'It isn't anything,' says Mrs. Bird, but even as she said that she could see a little hand holding fast to that cat's tail, and then the child seemed to sort of clear out of the dimness behind the hand, and the child was sort of laughing then, instead of looking sad, and she said that it was a great deal worse. She said that laugh was the most awful and the saddest thing she ever heard.

"Well, she was so dumbfounded that she didn't know what to do, and she couldn't sense at first that it was anything supernatural.

"'Don't you know that you mustn't pull the kitty's tail?' says she. 'Don't you know you hurt the poor kitty, and she'll scratch you if you don't take care. Poor kitty, you mustn't hurt her.'

"And with that she said the child stopped pulling the cat's tail and went to stroking her just as soft and pitiful, and the cat put his back up and rubbed and purred as if he liked it. The cat never seemed a mite afraid, and that seemed queer, for I had always heard that animals were dreadfully afraid of ghosts; but then, that was a pretty harmless little sort of ghost.

"Well, Mrs. Bird said the child stroked that cat, while she and Mrs. Dennison stood watching it, and holding onto each other, for, no matter how hard they tried to think it was all right, it didn't look right. Finally Mrs. Dennison spoke.

"'What's your name, little girl?' says she.

"Then the child looks up and stops stroking the cat, and says she can't find her mother, just the way she said it to me. 'Well, who is your mother?' says she. But the child just says again, 'I can't find my mother—I can't find my mother.'

"'Where do you live, dear?' says Mrs. Bird.

"'I can't find my mother,' says the child.

"Well, that was the way it was. Nothing happened. Those two women stood there hanging onto each other, and the child stood in front of them, and they asked her questions, and everything she would say was, 'I can't find my mother.'

"Then Mrs. Bird tried to catch hold of the child, for she thought, in spite of what she saw, that perhaps she was nervous and it was a real child, only perhaps not quite right in its head, that had run away in her little nightgown after she had been put to bed.

"She tried to catch the child. But the minute she moved toward the child there wasn't any child there; there was only that little voice seeming to come from nothing, saying, 'I can't find my mother,' and presently that died away.

"Well, that same thing kept happening, or something very much the same. Once in a while Mrs. Bird would be washing dishes, and all at once the child would be standing beside her with the dish towel, wiping them. Of course, that was terrible. Mrs. Bird would wash the dishes all over. Sometimes she didn't tell Mrs. Dennison, it made her so nervous. They never knew when they would come across that child, and always she kept saying over and over that she couldn't find her mother. They never tried talking to her, except once in awhile Mrs. Bird would get desperate and ask her something, but the child never seemed to hear it; she always kept right on saying that she couldn't find her mother.

"After they had told me all they had to tell about their experience with the child, they told me about the house and the people that had lived there before they did. It seemed something dreadful had happened in that house. And the land agent had never let on to them. I don't think they would have bought it if he had, no matter how cheap it was, for even if folks aren't really afraid of anything, they don't want to live in houses where such dreadful things have happened that you keep thinking about them."

"What was it?" asked Mrs. Emerson in an awed voice.

"It was an awful thing. That child had lived in the house with her father and mother two years before. They had come—or the father had—from a real good family. But the mother was a real wicked woman. She was as handsome as a picture, and they said she came from good enough sort of people in Boston, but she was bad clean through, though she was real pretty spoken and 'most everybody liked her. She used to dress out and make a great show, and she never seemed to take much interest in the child, and folks began to say she wasn't treated right.

"The woman had a hard time keeping a girl. For some reason one wouldn't stay. They would leave and then talk about her awfully, telling all kinds of things. People didn't believe it at first; then they began to. They said that the woman made that little thing, though she wasn't much over five years old, and small and babyish for her age, do most of the work, what there was done; they said the house used to look like a pigsty when she didn't have help. They said the little thing used to stand on a chair and wash dishes, and they'd seen her carrying in sticks of wood 'most as big as she was many a time, and they'd heard her mother scolding her.

"The father was away most of the time, and when that happened he had been away out West for some weeks. There had been a married man hanging about the mother for some time, and folks had talked some; but they weren't sure there was anything wrong, and he was a man very high up, with money, so they kept pretty still for fear he would hear of it and make trouble for them; and of course nobody was sure, though folks did say afterward that the father of the child had ought to have been told.

"But that was very easy to say; it wouldn't have been so easy to find anybody who would have been willing to tell him such a thing as that, especially when they weren't any too sure. He set his eyes by his wife, too. They said all he seemed to think of was to earn money to buy things to deck her out in. And he about worshipped the child, too. They said he was a real nice man. The men that are treated so bad mostly are real nice men. I've always noticed that.

"Well, one morning that man that there had been whispers about was missing. He had been gone quite a while, though, before they really knew that he was missing, because he had gone away and told his wife that he had to go to New York on business and might be gone a week, and not to worry if he didn't get home, and not to worry if he didn't write, because he should be thinking from day to day that he might take the next train home and there would be no use in writing. So the wife waited, and she tried not to worry until it was two days over the week, then she run into a neighbor's and fainted dead away on the floor; and then they made inquiries and found out that he had skipped—with some money that didn't belong to him, too.

"Then folks began to ask where was that woman, and

52

they found out by comparing notes that nobody had seen her since the man went away; but three or four women remembered that she had told them that she thought of taking the child and going to Boston to visit her folks, so when they hadn't seen her around, and the house shut, they jumped to the conclusion that was where she was. They were the neighbors that lived right around her, but they didn't have much to do with her, and she'd gone out of her way to tell them about her Boston plan.

"Well, there was this house shut up, and the man and woman missing and the child. Then all of a sudden one of the women that lived the nearest remembered something. She remembered that she had waked up three nights running, thinking she heard a child crying somewhere. She told what she had heard, and finally folks began to think they had better enter that house and see if there was anything wrong.

"Well, they did enter it, and they found that child dead, locked in one of the rooms. (Mrs. Dennison and Mrs. Bird never used that room; it was a back bedroom on the second floor.)

"Yes, they found that poor child there, starved to death, and frozen, though they weren't sure she had frozen to death, for she was in bed with clothes enough to keep her pretty warm when she was alive. But she had been there a week, and she was nothing but skin and bone. It looked as if the mother had locked her into the house when she went away, and told her not to make any noise for fear the neighbors would hear her and find out that she herself had gone.

"Mrs. Dennison said she couldn't really believe that the woman had meant to have her own child starved to death. Probably she thought the little thing would raise somebody, or folks would try to get in the house and find her. Well, whatever she thought, there the child was, dead.

"But that wasn't all. The father came home, right in the midst of it; the child was just buried, and he was beside himself. And—he went on the track of his wife, and he found her, and he shot her dead; it was in all the papers at the time; then he disappeared. Nothing had been seen of him since. Mrs. Dennison said that she thought he had either made away with himself or got out of the country, nobody knew, but they did know there was something wrong with the house.

"'I knew folks acted queer when they asked me how I liked it when we first came here,' says Mrs. Dennison, 'but I never dreamed why till we saw the child that night.'

"I never heard anything like it in my life," said Mrs. Emerson, staring at the other woman with awestruck eyes.

"I thought you'd say so," said Mrs. Meserve. "You don't wonder that I ain't disposed to speak light when I hear there is anything queer about a house, do you? But that ain't all."

"Did you see it again?" Mrs. Emerson asked.

"Yes, I saw it a number of times before the last time. It was lucky I wasn't nervous, or I never could have stayed there, much as I liked the place and much as I thought of those two women.

"Well, I stayed, and I never knew when I'd see that child. I got so I was very careful to bring everything of mine upstairs, and not leave any little thing in my room that needed doing, for fear she would come lugging up my coat or hat or gloves or I'd find things done when there'd been no live being in the room to do them. I can't tell you how I dreaded seeing her; and worse than the seeing her was the hearing her say, 'I can't find my mother.' It was enough to make your blood run cold. I never heard a living child cry for its mother that was anything so pitiful as that dead one. It was enough to break your heart.

"She used to come and say that to Mrs. Bird oftener than to anyone else. Once I heard Mrs. Bird say she wondered if it was possible that the poor little thing couldn't really find her mother in the other world, she had been such a wicked woman.

"But Mrs. Dennison told her she didn't think she ought to speak so nor even think so, and Mrs. Bird said she should not wonder if she was right. I don't think she was ever so scared by that poor little ghost, as much as she pitied it, and she was 'most heartbroken because she couldn't do anything for it, as she could have done for a live child.

"'It seems to me sometimes as if I should die if I can't get that awful little white robe off that child and get her in some clothes and feed her and stop her looking for her mother,' I heard her say once, and she was in earnest. She cried when she said it. That wasn't long before she died.

"Now I am coming to the strangest part of it all. Mrs. Bird died very sudden. One morning I went downstairs to breakfast, and Mrs. Bird wasn't there; there was nobody but Mrs. Dennison. She was pouring out the coffee when I came in. 'Why, where's Mrs. Bird?' says I.

"'Abby ain't feeling very well this morning,' says she; 'there isn't much the matter, I guess, but she didn't sleep very well, and her head aches, and she's sort of chilly, and I told her I thought she'd better stay in bed till the house gets warm.' It was a very cold morning.

"'Maybe she's got a cold,' says I.

"'Yes, I guess she has,' says Mrs. Dennison. 'I guess she's got a cold. She'll be up before long. Abby ain't one to stay in bed a minute longer than she can help.'

"Well, we went on eating our breakfast, and all at once a shadow flickered across one wall of the room and over the ceiling, the way a shadow will sometimes when somebody passes the window outside. Mrs. Dennison and I both looked up, then out of the window; then Mrs. Dennison she gives a scream.

"'Why, Abby's crazy!' says she. 'There she is out this bitter cold morning, and—and—' She didn't finish, but she meant the child. For we were both looking out, and we saw, as plain as we ever saw anything in our lives, Mrs. Abby Bird walking off over the white snowpath with that child holding fast to her hand, nestling close to her as if she had found her own mother.

"'She's dead,' says Mrs. Dennison, clutching hold of me hard. 'She's dead; my sister is dead!'

"She was. We hurried upstairs as fast as we could go, and she was dead in her bed, and smiling as if she was dreaming, and one arm and hand was stretched out as if something had hold of it; and it couldn't be straightened even at the last—it lay out over her casket at the funeral."

"Was the child ever seen again?" asked Mrs. Emerson in a shaking voice.

"No," replied Mrs. Meserve; "that child was never seen again after she went out of the yard with Mrs. Bird."

The Portrait-Painter's Story

by Charles Dickens

Considered the foremost writer of his time, CHARLES DICKENS had a gift for understanding the nature of people. He was born in Portsmouth, England, on February 7th, 1812, and moved to London when he was two. There, he dropped out of school when he was only fourteen, but he used his eye for observation to make up for what he lacked in education when writing his novels.

In the late 1820s Dickens became a writer for the London Evening Chronicle, and his first book, Sketches by Boz, published in 1836, came from articles he wrote for that newspaper.

But it was with the publication of The Posthumous Papers of the Pickwick Club, published in parts in 1836 and 1837, that Dickens became famous. And from that young age of twenty-four, he remained famous until his death from a stroke on June 9, 1870.

Recognized and revered all over England as well as the United States, Dickens unfortunately was not as successful in his personal life as he was in his professional one. In 1836 he married Catherine Hogarth. But a year later, when Catherine's sister, Mary, died, Dickens's immense grief over her death led many to believe that it was Mary Hogarth whom he actually loved. Nevertheless, Dickens and his wife had ten children before separating in 1858.

A man with enormous energy, Dickens spent his life writing,

editing, and touring as a dramatic reader. He also devoted many hours to charities involved with children and the poor, and much of his writing, including his most famous work, A Christmas Carol, was about those less fortunate.

In "The Portrait-Painter's Story," Dickens demonstrates his gift for understanding people when he writes compassionately about a young woman's desire to have her portrait painted in order to end her father's grief. The trick is, how can she contact the artist . . . from the grave?

I am a painter. One morning in May, 1858, I was seated in my studio at my usual occupation. At an earlier hour than that at which visits are usually made, I received one from a friend. It was incumbent on me to offer my visitor suitable refreshments; consequently, two o'clock found us well occupied in conversation, cigars, and a decanter of sherry. About that hour a ring at the bell reminded me of an engagement I had made with a model, or a young person who, having a pretty face and neck, earned a livelihood by sitting for artists. Not being in the humour for work, I arranged with her to come on the following day, promising, of course, to remunerate her for her loss of time, and she went away.

Close to the street in which I live there is another of a very similar name, and persons who are not familiar with my address often go to it by mistake. The model's way lay directly through it, and, on arriving there, she was accosted by a lady and gentleman who asked if she could inform them where I lived. They had forgotten my right address, and were endeavoring to find me by inquiring of persons whom they met; in a few more minutes they were shown into my room.

My new visitors were strangers to me. They had seen a

portrait I had painted, and wished for likenesses of themselves and their children. The price I named did not deter them, and they asked to look round the studio to select the style and size they should prefer. The inspection proving satisfactory, they asked whether I could paint the pictures at their house in the country, and there being no difficulty on this point, an engagement was made for the following autumn, subject to my writing to fix the time when I might be able to leave town for the purpose. This being adjusted, the gentleman gave me his card, and they left. Shortly afterwards my friend went also, and on looking for the first time at the card left by the strangers, I was somewhat disappointed to find that though it contained the name of Mr. and Mrs. Kirkbeck, there was no address. I tried to find it by looking at the Court Guide, but it contained no such name, so I put the card in my writing-desk, and forgot, for a time, the entire transaction.

Autumn came, and with it a series of engagements I had made in the north of England. Towards the end of September, 1858, I was one of a dinner party at a country house on the confines of Yorkshire and Lincolnshire. Being a stranger to the family, it was by a mere accident that I was at the house at all. I had arranged to pass a day and a night with a friend in the neighbourhood who was intimate at the house, and had received an invitation, and the dinner occurring on the evening in question, I had been asked to accompany him. The party was a numerous one, and as the meal approached its termination, and was about to subside into the dessert, the conversation became general. I should here mention that my hearing is defective; at some times more so than at others, and on this particular evening I was extra deaf—so much so, that the conversation only reached me in the form of a continued din. At one instant, however, I heard a word distinctly pronounced, though it was uttered by a person at a considerable distance from me, and that word was Kirkbeck. In the business of the London season I had forgotten all about the visitors of the spring, who had left their card without the address. The word reaching me under such circumstances, arrested my attention, and immediately recalled the transaction to my remembrance. On the first opportunity that offered, I asked a person whom I was conversing with if a family of the name in question was resident in the neighbourhood. I was told in reply, that a Mr. Kirkbeck lived at A—, at the farther end of the county. The next morning I wrote to this person, saying that I believed he called at my studio in the spring, and had made an arrangement with me, which I was prevented fulfilling by there being no address on his card. I gave as my address, The Post Office, York.

On applying there three days afterwards, I received a note from Mr. Kirkbeck, stating that he was very glad he had heard from me, and that if I would call on my return, he would arrange about the pictures; he also told me to write a day before I proposed coming, that he might not otherwise engage himself. It was ultimately arranged that I should go to his house the succeeding Saturday, stay till Monday morning, transact afterwards what matters I had to attend to in London, and return in a fortnight to execute the commissions.

The day having arrived for my visit, directly after breakfast I took my place in the morning train from York to London. The train would stop at Doncaster, and after that at Retford junction, where I should have to get out in order to take the line through Lincoln to A—. The day was cold, wet, foggy, and in every way as disagreeable as I have ever known a day to be in an English October. The carriage in which I was seated had no other occupant than myself, but at Doncaster a lady got in. I could see that the lady was young, certainly not more than two- or three-and-twenty; but being moderately tall, rather robust in make, and decided in expression, she might have been two or three years younger. I suppose that her complexion would be termed a medium one; her hair being of a bright brown, or auburn, while her eyes and rather decidedly marked eyebrows were nearly black. The colour of her cheek was of that pale transparent hue that sets off to such advantage large, expressive eyes, and an equable firm expression of mouth. On the whole, the ensemble was rather handsome than beautiful, her expression having that agreeable depth and harmony about it that rendered her face and features, though not strictly regular, infinitely more attractive than if they had been modeled upon the strictest rules of symmetry.

It is no small advantage on a wet day and a dull long journey to have an agreeable companion, one who can converse, and whose conversation has sufficient substance in it to make one forget the length and the dreariness of the journey. In this respect I had no deficiency to complain of, the lady being decidedly and agreeably conversational. When she had settled herself to her satisfaction, she asked to be allowed to look at my Bradshaw, and not being a proficient in that difficult work, she requested my aid in ascertaining at what time the train passed through Retford again on its way back from London to York. The conversation turned afterwards on general topics, and, somewhat to my surprise, she led it into such particular subjects as I might be supposed to be more especially familiar with; indeed, I could not avoid remarking that her entire manner, while it was anything but forward, was that of one who had either known me personally or by report. There was in her manner a kind of confidential reliance when she listened to me that is not usually accorded to a stranger, and sometimes she actually seemed to refer to different circumstances with which I had been connected in times past. After about three-quarters of an hour's conversation the train arrived at Retford, where I was to change carriages. On my alighting and wishing her good morning, she made a slight movement of the hand as if she meant me to shake it, and on my doing so she said, by way of adieu, "I dare say we shall meet again," to which I replied, "I hope that we shall all meet again," and so parted, she going on the line towards London, and I through Lincolnshire to A——. The remainder of the journey was cold, wet, and dreary. I missed the agreeable conversation, and tried to supply its place with a book I had brought with me from York, and the *Times* newspaper, which I had procured at Retford. But the most disagreeable journey comes to an end at last, and half-past five in the evening found me at the termination of mine. A carriage was waiting for me at the station, where Mr. Kirkbeck was also expected by the same train, but as he did not appear it was concluded he would come by the next—half an hour later; accordingly, the carriage drove away with myself only.

The family being from home at the moment, and the dinner hour being seven, I went at once to my room to unpack and to dress. Having completed these operations, I descended to the drawing-room. It probably wanted some time to the dinner hour, as the lamps were not lighted, but in their place a large blazing fire threw a flood of light into every corner of the room, and more especially over a lady who, dressed in deep black, was standing by the chimneypiece warming a very handsome foot on the edge of the fender. Her face being turned away from the door by which I had entered, I did not at first see her features; on my advancing into the middle of the room, however, the foot was immediately withdrawn, and she turned around to accost me, when, to my profound astonishment, I perceived that it was none other than my companion in the railway carriage. She betrayed no surprise at seeing me; on the contrary, with one of those agreeable joyous expressions that make the plainest woman appear beautiful, she accosted me with, "I said we should meet again."

My bewilderment at the moment almost deprived me of utterance. I knew of no railway or other means by which she could have come. I had certainly left her in a London train, and had seen it start, and the only conceivable way in which she could have come was by going on to Peterborough and then returning by a branch to A—, a circuit of about ninety miles. As soon as my surprise enabled me to speak, I said that I wished I had come by the same conveyance as herself.

"That would have been rather difficult," she rejoined.

At this moment the servant came with the lamps, and informed me that his master had just arrived and would be down in a few minutes.

The lady took up a book containing some engravings, and having singled one out (a portrait of Lady—), asked me to look at it well and tell her whether I thought it like her.

I was engaged trying to get up an opinion, when Mr. and Mrs. Kirkbeck entered, and shaking me heartily by the hand, apologized for not being at home to receive me; the gentleman ending by requesting me to take Mrs. Kirkbeck in to dinner.

The lady of the house having taken my arm, we marched on. The dinner party consisting of us four only, we fell into our respective places at the table without difficulty, the mistress and master of the house at the top and bottom, the lady in black and myself on each side. The dinner passed much as is usual on such occasions. I, having to play the guest, directed my conversation principally, if not exclusively, to my host and hostess, and I cannot call to mind that I or any one else once addressed the lady opposite. Seeing this, and remembering something that looked like a slight want of attention to her on coming into the dining room, I at once concluded that she was the governess.

The dinner ended, the ladies retired, and after the usual port, Mr. Kirkbeck and I joined them in the drawing room. By this time, however, a much larger party had assembled. Brothers and sisters-in-laws had come in from their residences in the neighbourhood, and several children, with Miss Hardwick, their governess, were also introduced to me. I saw at once that my supposition as to the lady in black being the governess was incorrect. After passing the time necessarily occupied in complimenting the children, and saying something to the different persons to whom I was introduced, I found myself again engaged in conversation with the lady of the railway carriage, and as the topic of the evening had referred principally to portrait-painting, she continued the subject.

"Do you think you could paint my portrait?" the lady inquired.

"Yes, I think I could, if I had the opportunity."

"Now, look at my face well; do you think you should recollect my features?"

"Yes, I am sure I should never forget your features."

"Of course I might have expected you to say that; but do you think you could do me from recollection?"

"Well, if it be necessary, I will try; but can't you give me any sittings?"

"No, quite impossible; it could not be. It is said that the print I showed to you before dinner is like me; do you think so?"

"Not much," I replied; "it has not your expression. If you can give me only one sitting, it would be better than none."

"No; I don't see how it could be."

The evening being by this time rather far advanced, and the chamber candles being brought in, on the plea of being rather tired, she shook me heartily by the hand, and wished me good night. My mysterious acquaintance caused me no small pondering during the night. I had never been introduced to her, I had not seen her speak to any one during the entire evening, not even to wish them good night—how she got across the country was an inexplicable mystery. Then, why did she wish me to paint her from memory, and why could she not give me even one sitting? Finding the difficulties of a solution to these questions rather increase upon me, I made up my mind to defer further consideration of them till breakfast time, when I supposed the matter would receive some elucidation.

The breakfast now came, but with it no lady in black. The breakfast over, we went to church, came home to luncheon, and so on through the day, but still no lady, neither any reference to her. I then concluded that she must be some relative, who had gone away early in the morning to visit another member of the family living close by. I was much puzzled, however, by no reference whatever being made to her, and finding no opportunity of leading any part of my conversation with the family towards the subject, I went to bed the second night more puzzled than ever.

On the servant coming in in the morning, I ventured to ask him the name of the lady who dined at the table on the Saturday evening, to which he answered, "A lady, sir? No lady, only Mrs. Kirkbeck, sir."

"Yes, the lady that sat opposite me dressed in black?"

"Perhaps, Miss Hardwick, the governess, sir?"

"No, not Miss Hardwick; she came down afterwards."

"No lady as I see, sir."

"Oh dear me, yes, the lady dressed in black that was in the drawing room when I arrived, before Mr. Kirkbeck came home?"

The man looked at me with surprise as if he doubted my sanity, and only answered, "I never see any lady, sir," and then left.

The mystery now appeared more impenetrable than ever—I thought it over in every possible aspect, but could come to no conclusion upon it. Breakfast was early that morning, in order to allow of my catching the morning train to London. The same cause also slightly hurried us, and allowed no time for conversation beyond that having direct reference to the business that brought me there; so, after arranging to return to paint the portraits on that day three weeks, I made my adieus, and took my departure for town.

It is only necessary for me to refer to my second visit to that house, in order to state that I was assured most positively, both by Mr. and Mrs. Kirkbeck, that no fourth person dined at the table on the Saturday evening in question.

Some weeks passed. It was close upon Christmas. The light of a short winter day was drawing to a close, and I was seated at my table, writing letters for the evening post. My back was towards the folding doors leading into the room in which my visitors usually waited. I had been engaged some minutes in writing, when, without hearing or seeing anything, I became aware that a person had come through the folding-doors, and was then standing beside me. I turned, and beheld the lady of the railway carriage. I suppose that my manner indicated that I was somewhat startled, as the lady, after the usual salutation, said, "Pardon me for disturbing you. You did not hear me come in." She asked me whether I had made any attempt at a likeness of her. I was obliged to confess that I had not. She regretted it much, as she wished one for her father. She had brought an engraving (a portrait of Lady M. A.) with her that she thought would assist me. It was like the one she asked my opinion upon at the house in Lincolnshire. It had always been considered very like her, and she would leave it with me. Then (putting her hand impressively on my arm) she added she really would be most thankful and grateful to me if I would do it (and, if I recollect rightly, she added), "*as much depended on it.*"

Seeing she was so much in earnest, I took up my sketch book, and by the dim light that was still remaining began to make a rapid pencil sketch of her. On observing my doing so, however, instead of giving me what assistance she was able, she turned away under pretense of looking at the pictures around the room, occasionally passing from one to another so as to enable me to catch a momentary glimpse of her features. In this manner I made two hurried but rather expressive sketches of her, which being all that the declining light would allow me to do, I shut my book, and she prepared to leave. This time, instead of the usual "Good morning," she wished me an impressively pronounced "Goodbye," firmly holding rather than shaking my hand while she said it. I accompanied her to the door, outside of which she seemed rather to fade into the darkness than to pass through it. But I refer this impression to my own fancy.

Soon after this occurred I had to fulfill an engagement at a house near Bosworth Field, in Leicestershire. I left town on a Friday, having sent some pictures, that were too large to take with me, by the luggage train a week previously, in order that they might be at the house on my arrival, and occasion me no loss of time in waiting for them. On getting to the house, however, I found that they had not been heard of, and on inquiring at the station, it was stated that a case similar to the one I described had passed through and gone on to Leicester, where it probably still was. It being Friday, and past the hour for the post, there was no possibility of getting a letter to Leicester before Monday morning, as the luggage office would be closed there on the Sunday. Consequently, I could in no case expect the arrival of the pictures before the succeeding Tuesday or Wednesday. The loss of three days would be a serious one; therefore, to avoid it, I suggested to my host that I should leave immediately to transact some business in South Staffordshire, as I should be obliged to attend to it before my return to town, and if I could see about it in the vacant interval thus thrown upon my hands, it would be saving me the same amount of time after my visit to his house was concluded. This arrangement meeting with his ready assent, I hastened to the Atherstone station on the Trent Valley Railway. By reference to Bradshaw, I found that my route lay through L—, where I was to change carriages, to S—, in Staffordshire. I was just in time for the train that would put me down at L— at eight in the evening, and a train was announced to start from L— for S— at ten minutes after eight, answering, as I concluded, to the train in which I was about to travel. I therefore saw no reason to doubt but that I should get to my journey's end the same night. But on my arriving at L—, I found my plans entirely frustrated. The train arrived punctually, and I got out intending to wait on the platform for the arrival of the carriages for the other line. I found, however, that though the two lines crossed at L—, they did not communicate with each other, the L— station on the Trent Valley line being on one side of the town, and the L— station on the South Staffordshire line on the other. I also found that there was not time to get to the other station so as to catch the train the same evening; indeed, the train had just that moment passed on a lower level beneath my feet, and to get to the other side of the town, where it would stop for two minutes only, was out of the question. There was, therefore, nothing for it but to put up at the Swan Hotel for the night.

This was the first time I had been in L—, and while waiting for the tea, it occurred to me how, on two occasions within the past six months, I had been on the point of coming to that very place, at one time to execute a small commission for an old acquaintance, resident there, and then another, to get the materials for a picture I proposed painting of an incident in the early life of Dr. Johnson. I should have come on each of these occasions had not other arrangements diverted my purpose and caused me to postpone the journey indefinitely. The thought, however, would occur to me, "How strange! Here I am at L—, by no intention of my own, though I have twice tried to get here and been balked." When I had done tea, I thought I might as well write to an acquaintance I had known some years previously, and who lived in the cathedral close, asking him to come and pass an hour or two with me. Accordingly, I rang for the waitress and asked, "Does Mr. Lute live in Lichfield?"

"Yes, sir."

"Cathedral close?"

"Yes, sir."

"Can I send a note to him?"

"Yes, sir."

I wrote the note, saying where I was, and asking if he would come for an hour or two and talk over old matters. The note was taken; in about twenty minutes a person of gentlemanly appearance, and what might be termed the advanced middle age, entered the room with my note in his hand, saying that I had sent him a letter, he presumed, by mistake, as he did not know my name. Seeing instantly that he was not the person I intended to write to, I apologized, and asked whether there was not another Mr. Lute living in L—?

"No, there was none other."

"Certainly," I rejoined, "my friend must have given me his right address, for I had written to him on other occasions here. He was a fair young man, he succeeded to an estate in consequence of his uncle having been killed while hunting with the Quorn hounds, and he married about two years since a lady of the name of Fairbairn."

The stranger very composedly replied, "You are speaking of Mr. Clyne; he did live in the cathedral close, but he has now gone away."

The stranger was right, and in my surprise I exclaimed, "Oh dear, to be sure, that is the name; what could have made me address you instead? I really beg your pardon; my writing to you, and unconsciously guessing your name, is one of the most extraordinary and unaccountable things I ever did. Pray pardon me."

He continued very quietly, "There is no need of apology; it happens that you are the very person I most wished to see. You are a painter, and I want you to paint a portrait of my daughter; can you come to my house immediately for the purpose?"

I was rather surprised at finding myself known to him, and the turn matters had taken being so entirely unexpected, I did not at the moment feel inclined to undertake the business. He, however, pressed me so earnestly, that I accompanied him to his house. During the walk home he scarcely spoke a word, but his taciturnity seemed only a continuance of his quiet composure at the inn. On our arrival he introduced me to his daughter Maria, and then left the room.

She had evidently not been informed of the purpose of my coming, and only knew that I was to stay there for the night; she therefore excused herself for a few moments, that she might give the requisite directions to the servants as to preparing my room. When she returned, she told me that I should not see her father again that evening, the state of his health having obliged him to retire for the night; but she hoped I should be able to see him some time on the morrow. In the meantime, she hoped I would make myself quite at home, and call for anything I wanted. She, herself, was sitting in the drawing room, but perhaps I should like to smoke and take something; if so, there was a fire in the housekeeper's room, and she would come and sit with me, as she expected the medical attendant every minute, and he would probably stay to smoke, and take something. As the little lady seemed to recommend this course, I readily complied. I did not smoke, or take anything, but sat down by the fire, when she immediately joined me. She conversed well and readily, and with a command of language singular in a person so young. Without being disagreeably inquisitive, or putting any question to me, she seemed desirous of learning the business that had brought me to the house. I told her that her father wished me to paint either her portrait or that of a sister of hers, if she had one.

She remained silent and thoughtful for a moment, and then seemed to comprehend it at once. She told me that a sister of hers, an only one, to whom her father was devotedly attached, died near four months previously; that her father had never yet recovered from the shock of her death. He had often expressed the most earnest wish for a portrait of her; indeed, it was his one thought, and she hoped, if something of the kind could be done, it would improve his health. Here she hesitated, stammered, and burst into tears. After a while she continued, "It is no use hiding from you what you must very soon be aware of. Papa is insane—he has been so ever since dear Caroline was buried. He says he is always seeing dear Caroline, and he is subject to fearful delusions. The doctor says he cannot tell how much worse he may be, and that everything dangerous, like knives or razors, are to be kept out of his reach. It was necessary you should not see him again this evening, as he was unable to converse properly, and I fear the same may be the case tomorrow; but perhaps you can stay over Sunday, and I may be able to assist you in doing what he wishes." I asked whether they had any materials for making a likeness—a photograph, a sketch, or anything else for me to go from. No, they had nothing. "Could she describe her clearly?" She thought she could; and there was a print that was very much like her, but she had mislaid it. I mentioned that with such disadvantages, and in such an absence of materials, I did not anticipate a satisfactory result. The medical attendant came, but I did not see him. I learnt, however, that he ordered a strict watch to be kept on his patient till he came again the next morning. Seeing the state of things, and how much the little lady had to attend to, I retired early to bed. The next morning I heard that her father was decidedly better; he had inquired earnestly on waking whether I was really in the house, and at breakfast time he sent down to say that he hoped nothing would prevent my making an attempt at the portrait immediately, and he expected to be able to see me in the course of the day.

Directly after breakfast I set to work, aided by such description as the sister could give me. I tried again and again, but without success, or, indeed, the least prospect of it. The features, I was told, were separately like, but the expression was not. I toiled on the greater part of the day with no better result. The different studies I made were taken up to the invalid, but the same answer was always returned—no resemblance. I had exerted myself to the utmost, and, in fact, was not a little fatigued by so doing—a circumstance that the little lady evidently noticed, as she expressed herself most grateful for the interest she could see I took in the matter, and referred the unsuccessful result entirely to her want of powers of description. She also said it was so provoking. She had a print—a portrait of a lady—that was so like, but it was gone—she had missed it from her book for three weeks past. It was the more disappointing, as she was sure it would have been of such great assistance. I asked if she could tell me who the print was of, as if I knew, I could easily procure one in London. She answered, Lady M. A. Immediately the name was uttered, the whole scene of the lady of the railway carriage presented itself to me. I had my sketch book in my portmanteau upstairs, and, by a fortunate chance, fixed in it was the print in question, with the two pencil sketches. I instantly brought them down, and showed them to Maria Lute. She looked at them for a moment, turned her eyes full upon me, and said slowly, and with something like fear in her manner, "Where did you get these?" Then quicker, and without waiting for my answer, "Let me take them instantly to papa." She was away ten minutes, or more. When she returned, her father came with her. He did not wait for salutations, but said, in a tone and manner I had not observed in him before, "I was right all the time; it was you that I saw with her, and these sketches are from her, and from no one else. I value them more than all my possessions, except this dear child." The daughter also assured me that the print I had brought to the house must be the one taken from the book about three weeks before, in proof of which she pointed out to me the gum marks at the back, which exactly corresponded with those left on the blank leaf. From the moment the father saw these sketches his mental health returned.

I was not allowed to touch either of the pencil drawings in the sketch book, as it was feared I might injure them; but an oil picture from them was commenced immediately, the father sitting by me hour after hour, directing my touches, conversing rationally, and indeed cheerfully, while he did so. He avoided direct reference to his delusions, but from time to time led the conversation to the manner in which I had originally obtained the sketches. The doctor came in the evening, and, after extolling the particular treatment he had adopted, pronounced his patient decidedly, and he believed permanently, improved.

The next day being Sunday, we all went to church; the father, for the first time since his bereavement. During a walk which he took with me after luncheon, he again approached the subject of the sketches, and after some seeming hesitation as to whether he should confide in me or not, said, "Your writing to me by name, from the inn at L—, was one of those inexplicable circumstances that I suppose it is impossible to clear up. I knew you, however, directly I saw you; when those about me considered that my intellect was disordered, and that I spoke incoherently, it was only because I saw things that they did not. Since her death, I know, with a certainty that nothing will ever disturb, that at different times I have been in the actual and visible presence of my dear daughter that is gone—oftener, indeed, just after her death than latterly. Of the many times that this has occurred, I distinctly remember once seeing her in a railway carriage, speaking to a person seated opposite; who that person was I could not ascertain, as my position seemed to be immediately behind him. I next saw her at a dinner table, with others, and amongst those others, unquestionably I saw yourself. I afterwards learnt that at the time I was considered to be in one of my longest and most violent paroxysms, as I continued to see her speaking to you, in the midst of a large assembly, for some hours. Again I saw her, standing by your side, while you were engaged in either writing or drawing. I saw her once again afterwards, but the next time I saw yourself was in the inn parlour."

The picture was proceeded with the next day, and on the

day after the face was completed, and I afterwards brought it with me to London to finish.

I have often seen Mr. L since that period; his health is perfectly re-established, and his manner and conversation are as cheerful as can be expected within a few years of so great a bereavement.

The portrait now hangs in his bedroom, with the print and the two sketches by the side, and written beneath is: "C. L., 13th September, 1858, aged 22."

THE CANTERVILLE GHOST

by Oscar Wilde

With a name like Oscar Fingal O'Flahertie Wills Wilde, it's no wonder that Irish born OSCAR WILDE (1856-1900) was known for his "wild" and outrageous ways—both in his artistic and personal life. In fact, while still a student at Oxford, the soon-to-be-famous author wrote, "Somehow or other I'll be famous, and if not famous, I'll be notorious."

True to his prediction, Wilde, with his long, wavy hair draped over fancy fur coats, grew infamous for his flamboyant ways, and was even once said to have engaged in contests of loud dress with the American painter James Whistler.

Wilde's literary fame began at twenty-three, with the publication of some of his poetry. Later, at thirty-two, his first collection of fiction, The Happy Prince and Other Tales, was printed, and at thirty-nine, one of his most famous plays, The Importance of Being Earnest, was produced in London at the St. James Theater. His favorite theme was challenging social conventions, and he did so with enthusiasm in perhaps his most famous work, The Picture of Dorian Gray, a novel published in 1891.

Once engaged to Bram Stoker's wife, Florence Balcombe, Wilde eventually married Constance Lloyd in 1883 and raised a family. But as he grew older, Wilde's lifestyle became increasingly reckless, and toward the end of his life he had become obese and had taken to excessive drinking.

"Sometimes I think that the artistic life is a long and lovely suicide," Wilde said of his deterioration, *"and I am not sorry that it is so."* Not surprisingly, Wilde, his mind and body weakened to the point of exhaustion, died on November 30, 1900, at the young age of forty-four, of what most believe was a disease of the inner ear.

This excerpt from the spooky, yet humorous, story "The Canterville Ghost" turns the tables on just who is scaring whom while, at the same time, it pokes fun at American ideals.

I

When Mr. Hiriam B. Otis, the American Minister, bought Canterville Chase, everyone told him he was doing a very foolish thing, as there was no doubt at all that the place was haunted. Indeed, Lord Canterville himself, who was a man of the most punctilious honour, had felt it his duty to mention the fact to Mr. Otis when they came to discuss terms.

"We have not cared to live in the place ourselves," said Lord Canterville, "since my grand-aunt, the Dowager Duchess of Bolton, was frightened into a fit, from which she never really recovered, by two skeleton hands being placed on her shoulders as she was dressing for dinner, and I feel bound to tell you, Mr. Otis, that the ghost has been seen by several living members of my family, as well as by the rector of the parish, the Rev. Augustus Dampier, who is a Fellow of King's College, Cambridge. After the unfortunate accident to the Duchess, none of our younger servants would stay with us, and Lady Canterville often got very little sleep at night, in consequence of the mysterious noises that came from the corridor and the library."

"My Lord," answered the Minister, "I will take the furniture and the ghost at a valuation. I come from a modern country, where we have everything that money can buy; and with all our spry young fellows painting the Old World red, and carrying off your best actresses and prima donnas, I reckon that if there were such a thing as a ghost in Europe, we'd have it at home in a very short time in one of our public museums, or on the road as a show."

"I fear that the ghost exists," said Lord Canterville, smiling, "though it may have resisted the overtures of your enterprising impresarios. It has been well known for three centuries, since 1584 in fact, and always makes its appearance before the death of any member of our family."

"Well, so does the family doctor, for that matter, Lord Canterville. But there is no such thing, sir, as a ghost, and I guess the laws of Nature are not going to be suspended for the British aristocracy."

"You are certainly very natural in America," answered Lord Canterville, who did not quite understand Mr. Otis's last observation, "and if you don't mind a ghost in the house, it is all right. Only you must remember I warned you."

A few weeks after this the purchase was completed, and at the close of the season, the Minister and his family went down to Canterville Chase. Mrs. Otis was a very handsome, middle-aged woman, with fine eyes, and a superb profile. Her eldest son, christened Washington by his parents in a moment of patriotism, which he never ceased to regret, was a fair-haired, rather good-looking young man. Miss Virginia E. Otis was a little girl of fifteen, lithe and lovely as a fawn, and with a fine freedom in her large, blue eyes. She was a wonderful amazon, and had once raced old Lord Bilton on her pony twice round the park, winning by a length and a half, just in front of the Achilles statue; to the huge delight of the young Duke of Cheshire, who proposed to her on the spot, and was sent back to Eton that very night by his guardians, in floods of tears. After Virginia came the twins. They were delightful boys, and, with the exception of the worthy Minister, the only true republicans of the family.

As Canterville Chase is seven miles from Ascot, the nearest railway station, Mr. Otis had telegraphed for a wagonette to meet them, and they started on their drive in high spirits. It was a lovely July evening, and the air was delicate with the scent of the pinewoods. As they entered the avenue of Canterville Chase, however, the sky became suddenly overcast with clouds, a curious stillness seemed to hold the atmosphere, a great flight of rooks passed silently over their heads, and, before they reached the house, some big drops of rain had fallen.

Standing on the steps to receive them was an old woman, neatly dressed in black silk, with a white cap and apron. This was Mrs. Umney, the housekeeper, whom Mrs. Otis, at Lady Canterville's earnest request, had consented to keep on in her former position. She made them each a low curtsy as they alighted, and said in a quaint, old-fashioned manner, "I bid you welcome to Canterville Chase." Following her, they passed through the fine Tudor hall into the library, a long, low room, paneled in black oak, at the end of which was a large stained-glass window. Here they found tea laid out for them, and, after taking off their wraps, they sat down and began to look around, while Mrs. Umney waited on them.

Suddenly Mrs. Otis caught sight of a dull red stain on the floor just by the fireplace and, quite unconscious of what it really signified, said to Mrs. Umney, "I am afraid something has been spilt there."

"Yes, madam," replied the housekeeper in a low voice, "blood has been spilt on that spot."

"How horrid," cried Mrs. Otis; "I don't at all care for blood-stains in a sitting-room. It must be removed at once."

The old woman smiled, and answered in the same low, mysterious voice, "It is the blood of Lady Eleanore de Canterville, who was murdered on that very spot by her own husband, Sir Simon de Canterville, in 1575. Sir Simon survived her nine years, and disappeared suddenly under very mysterious circumstances. His body has never been discovered, but his guilty spirit still haunts the Chase. The blood-stain has been much admired by tourists and others, and cannot be removed."

"That is all nonsense," cried Washington Otis; "Pinkerton's Champion Stain Remover and Paragon Detergent will clean it up in no time," and before the terrified housekeeper could interfere he had fallen upon his knees, and was rapidly scouring the floor with a small stick of what looked like a black cosmetic. In a few moments no trace of the bloodstain could be seen.

"I knew Pinkerton would do it," he exclaimed triumphantly, as he looked round at his admiring family; but no sooner had he said these words than a terrible flash of lightning lit up the somber room, a fearful peal of thunder made them all start to their feet, and Mrs. Umney fainted.

"My dear Hiram," cried Mrs. Otis, "what can we do with a woman who faints?"

"Charge it to her, like breakages," answered the Minister; "she won't faint after that"; and in a few moments Mrs. Umney certainly came to. There was no doubt, however, that she was extremely upset, and she sternly warned Mr. Otis to beware of some trouble coming to the house.

"I have seen things with my own eyes, sir," she said, "that would make any Christian's hair stand on end, and many and many a night I have not closed my eyes in sleep for the awful things that are done here." Mr. Otis, however, and his wife warmly assured the honest soul that they were not afraid of ghosts, and, after invoking the blessings of Providence on her new master and mistress, and making arrangements for an increase of salary, the old housekeeper tottered off to her own room.

II

The storm raged fiercely all that night, but nothing of particular note occurred. The next morning, however, when they came down to breakfast, they found the terrible stain of blood once again on the floor. "I don't think it can be the fault of the Paragon Detergent," said Washington, "for I have tried it with everything. It must be the ghost." He accordingly rubbed out the stain a second time, but the second morning it appeared again. The third morning also it was there, though the library had been locked up at night by Mr. Otis himself, and the key carried upstairs. The whole family was now quite interested; Mr. Otis began to suspect that he had been too dogmatic in his denial of the existence of ghosts, Mrs. Otis expressed her intention of joining the Psychical Society, and Washington prepared a long letter to Messrs. Myers and Podmore on the subject of the Permanence of Sanguineous

Stains when connected with Crime. That night all doubts about the objective existence of phantasmata were removed forever.

The day had been warm and sunny; and, in the cool of the evening, the whole family went out for a drive. They did not return home till nine o'clock, when they had a light supper. No mention at all was made of the supernatural, nor was Sir Simon de Canterville alluded to in any way. At eleven o'clock the family retired, and by half-past all the lights were out. Some time after, Mr. Otis was awakened by a curious noise in the corridor, outside his room. It sounded like the clank of metal, and seemed to be coming nearer every moment. He got up at once, struck a match, and looked at the time. It was exactly one o'clock. He was quite calm, and felt his pulse, which was not at all feverish. The strange noise still continued, and with it he heard distinctly the sound of footsteps. He put on his slippers, took a small oblong phial out of his dressing-case, and opened the door. Right in front of him he saw, in the wan moonlight, an old man of terrible aspect. His eyes were as red as burning coals; his garments, which were of antique cut, were soiled and ragged and from his wrists and ankles hung heavy manacles and rusty gyves.

"My dear sir," said Mr. Otis, "I really must insist on your oiling those chains, and have brought you for that purpose a small bottle of the Tammany Rising Sun Lubricator. I shall leave it here for you by the bedroom candles, and will be happy to supply you with more should you require it." With these words the United States Minister laid the bottle down on a marble table, and, closing his door, retired to rest.

For a moment the Canterville ghost stood quite motionless in natural indignation; then, dashing the bottle violently upon the polished floor, he fled down the corridor, uttering hollow groans, and emitting a ghastly green light. Just, however, as he reached the top of the great oak staircase, a door was flung open, two little white-robed figures appeared, and a large pillow whizzed past his head! There was evidently no time to be lost, so, hastily adopting the Fourth Dimension of Space as a means of escape, he vanished through the wainscoting, and the house became quite quiet.

On reaching a small, secret chamber in the left wing, he leaned up against a moonbeam to recover his breath, and began to try and realize his position. Never, in a brilliant and uninterrupted career of three hundred years, had he been so grossly insulted. He thought of the Dowager Duchess, whom he had frightened into a fit as she stood before the glass in her lace and diamonds, and of old Madame de Tremouillac, who, having wakened up one morning early and seen a skeleton seated in an arm-chair by the fire reading her diary, had been confined to her bed for six weeks with an attack of brain fever, and, on her recovery, had become reconciled to the Church, and broken off her connection with that notorious skeptic Monsieur de Voltaire. He remembered the terrible night when the wicked Lord Canterville was found choking in his dressing-room, with a knave of diamonds halfway down his throat, and confessed, just before he died, that he had cheated Charles James Fox out of £50,000 at Crockford's by means of that very card, and swore that the ghost had made him swallow it. With the enthusiastic egotism of the true artist he went over his most celebrated performances, and smiled bitterly to himself as he recalled to mind his last appearance as "Red Ruben, or the Strangled Babe," his debut as "Gaunt Gibeon, the Blood-sucker of Bexley Moor," and the furor he had excited, one lovely June evening, by merely playing ninepins with his own bones upon the lawn-tennis ground. And after all this, some wretched modern Americans were to come and offer him the Rising Sun Lubricator, and throw pillows at his head! It was quite unbearable. Besides, no ghosts in history had ever been treated in this manner. Accordingly, he determined to have vengeance, and remained till daylight in an attitude of deep thought.

III

The next morning when the Otis family met at breakfast, they discussed the ghost at some length. The United States Minister was naturally a little annoyed to find that his present had not been accepted. "I have no wish," he said, "to do the ghost any personal injury, and I must say that, considering the length of time he has been in the house, I don't think it is at all polite to throw pillows at him"—a very just remark, at which, I am sorry to say, the twins burst into shouts of laughter. "Upon the other hand," he continued, "if he really declines to use the Rising Sun Lubricator, we shall have to take his chains from him. It would be quite impossible to sleep with such a noise going on outside the bedrooms."

For the rest of the week, however, they were undisturbed, the only thing that excited any attention being the continual renewal of the bloodstain on the library floor. This certainly was very strange, as the door was always locked at night by Mr. Otis, and the windows kept closely barred. The chameleon-like colour, also, of the stain excited a good deal of comment. Some mornings it was a dull (almost Indian) red, then it would be vermilion, then a rich purple, and once when they came down for family prayers, they found it a bright emerald-green. These kaleidoscopic changes naturally amused the party very much, and bets on the subject were freely made every evening. The only person who did not enter into the joke was little Virginia, who, for some unexplained reason, was always a good deal distressed at the sight of the bloodstain, and very nearly cried the morning it was emerald-green.

The second appearance of the ghost was on Sunday night. Shortly after they had gone to bed they were suddenly alarmed by a fearful crash in the hall. Rushing downstairs, they found that a large suit of old armour had become detached from its stand, and had fallen on the stone floor, while seated in a high-backed chair was the Canterville ghost, rubbing his knees with an expression of acute agony on his face. The twins, having brought their pea-shooters with them, at once discharged two pellets at him with that accuracy of aim which can only be attained by long and careful practice on a writing-master, while the United States Minister covered him with his revolver, and called upon him, in accordance with Californian etiquette, to hold up his hands! The ghost started up with a wild shriek of rage, and swept through them like a mist, extinguishing Washington Otis's candle as he passed, and so leaving them all in total darkness. On reaching the top of the staircase he recovered himself, and determined to give his celebrated peal of demoniac laughter. This he had on more than one occasion found extremely useful. It was said to have turned Lord Raker's wig gray in a single night, and had certainly made three of Lady Canterville's French governesses give warning before their month was up. He accordingly laughed his most horrible laugh, till the old vaulted roof rang and rang again, but hardly had the fearful echo died away when a door opened, and Mrs. Otis came out in a light blue dressing-gown. "I am afraid you are far from well," she said, "and have brought you a bottle of Dr. Dobell's tincture. If it is indigestion, you will find it a most excellent remedy." The ghost glared at her in fury, and began at once to make preparations for turning himself into a large black dog, an accomplishment for which he was justly renowned, and to which the family doctor always attributed the permanent idiocy of Lord Canterville's uncle, the Hon. Thomas Horton. The sound of approaching footsteps, however, made him hesitate in his fell purpose, so he contented himself with becoming faintly phosphorescent, and vanished with a deep, churchyard groan, just as the twins had come up to him.

On reaching his room he entirely broke down, and became a prey to the most violent agitation. The vulgarity of the twins, and the gross materialism of Mrs. Otis, were naturally extremely annoying, but what really distressed him most was, that he had been unable to wear the suit of mail. He had hoped that even modern Americans would be thrilled by the sight of a Spectre In Armour, if for no more sensible reason, at least out of respect for their national poet, Longfellow, over whose graceful and attractive poetry he himself had whiled away many a weary hour when the Cantervilles were up in town. Besides, it was his own suit. He had worn it with great success at the Kenilworth tournament, and had been highly complimented on it by no less a person than the Virgin Queen herself. Yet when he had put it on he had been completely overpowered by the weight of the huge breastplate and steel casque, and had fallen heavily on the stone pavement.

For some days after this he was extremely ill, and hardly

stirred out of his room at all, except to keep the bloodstain in proper repair. However, by taking great care of himself, he recovered, and resolved to make a third attempt to frighten the United States Minister and his family. His plan of action was this. He was to make his way quietly to Washington Otis's room, gibber at him from the foot of the bed, and stab himself three times in the throat to the sound of slow music. He bore Washington a special grudge, being quite aware that it was he who was in the habit of removing the famous Canterville bloodstain, by means of Pinkerton's Paragon Detergent. Having reduced the reckless and foolhardy youth to a condition of abject terror, he was then to proceed to the room occupied by the United States Minister and his wife, and there to place a clammy hand on Mrs. Otis's forehead, while he hissed into her trembling husband's ear the awful secrets of the charnel-house. With regard to little Virginia, he had not quite made up his mind. She had never insulted him in any way, and was pretty and gentle. A few hollow groans from the wardrobe, he thought, would be more than sufficient, or, if that failed to wake her, he might grabble at the counterpane with palsy-twitching fingers. As for the twins, he was quite determined to teach them a lesson. The first thing to be done was, of course, to sit upon their chests, so as to produce the stifling sensation of nightmare. Then, as their beds were quite close to each other, to stand between them in the form of a green, icy-cold corpse, till they became paralyzed with fear, and finally, to throw off the winding-sheet, and crawl round the room, with white, bleached bones and one rolling eyeball.

At half-past ten he heard the family going to bed. For some time he was disturbed by wild shrieks of laughter from the twins, who, with the light-hearted gaiety of schoolboys, were evidently amusing themselves before they retired to rest, but at a quarter past eleven all was still, and, as midnight sounded, he sallied forth. The owl beat against the window panes, the raven croaked from the old yew tree, and the wind wandered moaning round the house like a lost soul; but the Otis family slept unconscious of their doom, and high above the rain and storm he could hear the steady snoring of the Minister for the United States. He stepped stealthily out of the wainscoting, with an evil smile on his cruel, wrinkled mouth, and the moon hid her face in a cloud as he stole past the great oriel window, where his own arms and those of his murdered wife were blazoned in azure and gold. On and on he glided, like an evil shadow, the very darkness seeming to loathe him as he passed. Finally he reached the corner of the passage that led to luckless Washington's room. For a moment he paused there, the wind blowing his long gray locks about his head, and twisting into grotesque and fantastic folds the nameless horror of the dead man's shroud. Then the clock struck the quarter, and he felt the time was come. He chuckled to himself, and turned the corner; but no sooner had he done so, than, with a piteous wail of terror, he fell back, and hid his blanched face in his long, bony hands. Right in front of him was standing a horrible spectre, motionless as a carven image, and monstrous as a madman's dream! On its breast was a placard with strange writing in antique characters, some scroll of shame it seemed, some record of wild sins, some awful calendar of crime, and, with its right hand, it bore aloft a falchion of gleaming steel.

Never having seen a ghost before, he naturally was terribly frightened, and, after a second hasty glance at the awful phantom, he fled back to his room, tripping up in his long winding-sheet as he sped down the corridor, and finally dropping the rusty dagger into the Minister's jackboots, where it was found in the morning by the butler. Once in the privacy of his own apartment, he flung himself down on a small pallet-bed, and hid his face under the clothes. After a time, however, the brave old Canterville spirit asserted itself, and he determined to go and speak to the other ghost as soon as it was daylight. Accordingly, just as the dawn was touching the hills with silver, he returned towards the spot where he had first laid eyes on the grisly phantom, feeling that, after all, two ghosts were better than one, and that, by the aid of his new friend, he might safely grapple with the twins. On reaching the spot, however, a terrible sight met his gaze. Something had evidently happened to the spectre, for the light had entirely faded from its hollow eyes, the gleaming falchion had fallen from its hand, and it was leaning up against the wall in a strained and uncomfortable attitude. He rushed forward and seized it in his arms, when, to his horror, the head slipped off and rolled on the floor, the body assumed a recumbent posture, and he found himself clasping a white dimity bed-curtain, with a sweeping-brush, a kitchen cleaver, and a hollow turnip lying at his feet! Unable to understand this curious transformation, he clutched the placard with feverish haste, and there, in the gray morning light, he read these fearful words:

YE OTIS GHOST.
Ye Onlie True and Originale Spook,
BEWARE OF YE IMITATIONES.
ALL OTHERS ARE COUNTERFEITS.

The whole thing flashed across him. He had been tricked, foiled, and outwitted! The old Canterville look came into his eyes; he ground his toothless gums together; and, raising his withered hands high above his head, swore, according to the picturesque phraseology of the antique school, that when Chanticleer had sounded twice his merry horn, deeds of blood would be wrought, and Murder walk abroad with silent feet.

Hardly had he finished this awful oath when, from the red-tiled roof of a distant homestead, a cock crew. He laughed a long, low, bitter laugh, and waited. Hour after hour he waited, but the cock, for some strange reason, did not crow again. Finally, at half-past seven, the arrival of the housemaids made him give up his fearful vigil, and he stalked back to his room, thinking of his vain hope and baffled purpose. There he consulted several books on ancient chivalry, of which he was exceedingly fond, and found that, on every occasion on which his oath had been used, Chanticleer had always crowed a second time. "Perdition seize the naughty fowl," he muttered. "I have seen the day when, with my stout spear, I would have run him through the gorge, and made him crow for me an 'twere in death!" He then retired to a comfortable lead coffin, and stayed there till evening.

IV

The next day the ghost was very weak and tired. The terrible excitement of the last four weeks was beginning to have its effect. His nerves were completely shattered, and he started at the slightest noise. For five days he kept to his room, and at last made up his mind to give up the point of the bloodstain on the library floor. If the Otis family did not want it, they

clearly did not deserve it. The question of phantasmic apparitions, and the development of astral bodies, was, of course,
quite a different matter, and really not under his control. It
was his solemn duty to appear in the corridor once a week,
and to gibber from the large oriel window on the first and
third Wednesday in every month, and he did not see how he
could honourably escape from his obligations. It is quite true
that his life had been very evil, but, upon the other hand, he
was most conscientious in all things connected with the
supernatural. For the next three Saturdays, accordingly, he
traversed the corridor as usual between midnight and three
o'clock, taking every possible precaution against being either
heard or seen. He removed his boots, trod as lightly as possible on the old, worm-eaten boards, wore a large black velvet
cloak, and was careful to use the Rising Sun Lubricator for
oiling his chains. He felt a little humiliated at first, but afterwards was sensible enough to see that there was a great deal
to be said for the invention, and, to a certain degree, it served
his purpose. Still, in spite of everything, he was not left
unmolested. He now gave up all hope of ever frightening this
rude American family, and contented himself, as a rule, with
creeping about the passages in slippers, with a thick red
muffler round his throat for fear of draughts, and a small
arquebus, in case he should be attacked by the twins. The
final blow he received occurred on the 19th of September. It
was about a quarter past two o'clock in the morning, and, as
far as he could ascertain, no one was stirring. As he was
strolling towards the library, however, to see if there were any
traces left of the bloodstain, suddenly there leaped out on him
from a dark corner two figures, who waved their arms wildly
above their heads, and shrieked out "BOO!" in his ear.

Seized with a panic, which, under the circumstances, was only natural, he rushed for the staircase, but found Washington Otis waiting for him there with the big garden-syringe; and being thus hemmed in by his enemies on every side, and driven almost to bay, he vanished into the great iron stove, which, fortunately for him, was not lit, and had to make his way home through the flues and chimneys, arriving at his own room in a terrible state of dirt, disorder, and despair.

After this he was not seen again on any nocturnal expedition. It was generally assumed that the ghost had gone away, and, in fact, Mr. Otis wrote a letter to that effect to Lord Canterville, who, in reply, expressed his great pleasure at the news, and sent his best congratulations to the Minister's worthy wife.

The Otises, however, were deceived, for the ghost was still in the house, and, though now almost an invalid, was by no means ready to let the matter rest, particularly as he heard that among the guests was the young Duke of Cheshire, whose grand-uncle, Lord Francis Stilton, had once bet a hundred guineas with Colonel Carbury that he would play dice with the Canterville ghost, and was found the next morning lying on the floor of the card-room in such a helpless paralytic state, that though he lived on to a great age, he was never able to say anything again but "Double Sixes." The ghost, then, was naturally very anxious to show that he had not lost his influence over the Stiltons, with whom, as everyone knows, the Dukes of Cheshire are lineally descended. Accordingly, he made arrangement for appearing to Virginia's little lover in his celebrated impersonation of "The Vampire Monk, or the Bloodless Benedictine." At the last moment, however, his terror of the twins prevented his leaving his room, and the little

Duke slept in peace under the great feathered canopy in the Royal Bedchamber, and dreamed of Virginia.

V

A few days after this, Virginia and her curly-haired cavalier went out riding on Brockley meadows, where she tore her habit so badly in getting through a hedge, that, on her return home, she made up her mind to go up by the back staircase so as not to be seen. As she was running past the Tapestry Chamber, the door of which happened to be open, she fancied she saw someone inside, and thinking it was her mother's maid, who sometimes used to bring her work there, looked in to ask her to mend her habit. To her immense surprise, however, it was the Canterville Ghost himself! His head was leaning on his hand, and his whole attitude was one of extreme depression. Indeed, so forlorn, and so much out of repair did he look, that little Virginia, whose first idea had been to run away and lock herself in her room, was filled with pity, and determined to try to comfort him. So light was her footfall, and so deep his melancholy, that he was not aware of her presence until she spoke to him.

"I am so sorry for you," she said, "but my brothers are going back to Eton tomorrow, and then, if you behave yourself, no one will annoy you."

"It is absurd asking me to behave myself," he answered, looking round in astonishment at the pretty little girl who had ventured to address him, "quite absurd. I must rattle my chains, and groan through keyholes, and walk about at night, if that is what you mean. It is my only reason for existing."

"It is no reason at all for existing, and you know you have been very wicked. Mrs. Umney told us, the first day we arrived here, that you had killed your wife."

"Well, I quite admit it," said the Ghost petulantly, "but it was a purely family matter, and concerned with no one else."

"It is very wrong to kill anyone," said Virginia, who at times had a sweet Puritan gravity, caught from some old New England ancestor.

"Oh, I hate the cheap severity of abstract ethics! My wife was very plain, never had my ruffs properly starched, and knew nothing about cookery. Why, there was a buck I had shot in Hogley Woods, a magnificent pricket, and do you know how she had it sent up to table? However, it is no matter now, for it is all over, and I don't think it was very nice of her brothers to starve me to death, though I did kill her."

"Starve you to death? Oh, Mr. Ghost, I mean Sir Simon, are you hungry? I have a sandwich in my case. Would you like it?"

"No, thank you, I never eat anything now; but it is very kind of you, all the same, and you are much nicer than the rest of your horrid, rude, vulgar, dishonest family."

"Stop!" cried Virginia, stamping her foot, "it is you who are rude, and horrid, and vulgar, and as for dishonesty, you know you stole the paints out of my box to try and furbish up that ridiculous bloodstain in the library. First you took all my reds, including the vermilion, and I couldn't do any more sunsets, and then you took the emerald-green and the chrome-yellow, and finally I had nothing left but indigo and Chinese white, and could only do moonlight scenes, which are always depressing to look at, and not at all easy to paint. I never told on you, though I was very much annoyed, and it was most ridiculous, the whole thing; for who ever heard of emerald-green blood?"

"Well, really," said the Ghost, rather meekly, "what was I to do? It is a very difficult thing to get real blood nowadays, and, as your brother began it all with his Paragon Detergent, I certainly saw no reason why I should not have your paints. As for colour, that is always a matter of taste; the Cantervilles have blue blood, for instance, the very bluest in England; but I know you Americans don't care for things of this kind."

"You know nothing about it, and the best thing you can do is to emigrate and improve your mind. My father will be only too happy to give you a free passage, and though there is a heavy duty on spirits of every kind, there will be no difficulty about the Custom House, as the officers are all Democrats. Once in New York, you are sure to be a great success. I know lots of people there who would give a hundred thousand dollars to have a grandfather, and much more than that to have a family Ghost."

"I don't think I should like America."

"I suppose because we have no ruins and no curiosities," said Virginia satirically.

"No ruins! No curiosities!" answered the Ghost; "you have your navy and your manners."

"Good evening; I will go and ask papa to get the twins an extra week's holiday."

"Please don't go, Miss Virginia," he cried; "I am so lonely and so unhappy, and I really don't know what to do. I want to go to sleep and I cannot."

"That's quite absurd! You have merely to go to bed and blow out the candle. It is very difficult, sometimes, to keep awake, especially at church, but there is no difficulty at all about sleeping. Why, even babies know how to do that, and they are not very clever."

"I have not slept for three hundred years," he said sadly, and Virginia's beautiful blue eyes opened in wonder; "for three hundred years I have not slept, and I am so tired."

Virginia grew quite grave, and her little lips trembled like rose-leaves. She came toward him, and kneeling down at his side, looked up into his old, withered face.

"Poor, poor Ghost," she murmured; "have you no place where you can sleep?"

"Far away beyond the pine-woods," he answered, in a low dreamy voice, "there is a little garden. There the grass grows long and deep, there are the great white stars of the hemlock flower, there the nightingale sings all night long. All night long he sings, and the cold, crystal moon looks down, and the yew tree spreads out its giant arms over the sleepers."

Virginia's eyes grew dim with tears, and she hid her face in her hands. "You mean the Garden of Death," she whispered.

"Yes, Death. Death must be so beautiful. To lie in the soft, brown earth, with the grasses waving above one's head, and listen to silence. To have no yesterday, and no tomorrow. To forget time, to forgive life, to be at peace. You can help me. You can open for me the portals of Death's house, for Love is always with you, and Love is stronger than Death is."

Virginia trembled, a cold shudder ran through her, and for a few moments there was silence. She felt as if she was in a terrible dream.

Then the Ghost spoke again. "Have you ever read the old prophecy on the library window?"

"Oh, often," cried the little girl, looking up; "I know it quite well. It is painted in curious black letters, and it is difficult to read. There are only six lines:

> *When a golden girl can win*
> *Prayer from out of the lips of sin,*
> *When the barren almond bears,*
> *And a little child gives away its tears,*
> *Then shall all the house be still*
> *And peace come to Canterville.*

"But I don't know what they mean."

"They mean," he said sadly, "that you must weep for me for my sins, because I have no tears, and pray with me for my soul, because I have no faith, and then, if you have always been sweet, and good, and gentle, the Angel of Death will have mercy on me."

Virginia made no answer, and the Ghost wrung his hands in wild despair as he looked down at her bowed golden head. Suddenly she stood up, very pale, and with a strange light in her eyes. "I am not afraid," she said firmly, "and I will ask the Angel to have mercy on you."

He rose from his seat with a faint cry of joy, and taking her hand bent over it with old-fashioned grace and kissed it. His fingers were as cold as ice, and his lips burned like fire, but Virginia did not falter, as he led her across the dusky room. On the faded green tapestry were broidered little huntsmen. They blew their tasseled horns, and with their tiny hands waved to her to go back. "Go back! little Virginia," they cried, "go back!" but the Ghost clutched her hand more tightly, and she shut her eyes against them. Horrible animals with lizard tails, and goggle eyes, blinked at her from the carven chimneypiece, and murmured, "Beware! little Virginia, beware! we may never see you again," but the Ghost glided on more swiftly, and Virginia did not listen. When they reached the end of the room he stopped, and muttered some

100

words she could not understand. She opened her eyes, and saw the wall slowly fading away like a mist, and a great black cavern in front of her. A bitter cold wind swept round them, and she felt something pulling at her dress. "Quick, quick," cried the Ghost, "or it will be too late," and, in a moment, the wainscoting had closed behind them, and the Tapestry Chamber was empty.

VI

About ten minutes later the bell rang for tea, and, as Virginia did not come down, Mrs. Otis sent up one of the footmen to tell her. After a little time he returned and said that he could not find Miss Virginia anywhere. As she was in the habit of going out to the garden every evening to get flowers for the dinner-table, Mrs. Otis was not at all alarmed at first, but when six o'clock struck, and Virginia did not appear, she became really agitated, and sent the boys out to look for her while she herself and Mr. Otis searched every room in the house. At half-past six the boys came back and said that they could find no trace of their sister anywhere. They were all now in the greatest state of excitement, and did not know what to do, when Mr. Otis suddenly remembered that, some few days before, he had given a band of gypsies permission to camp in the park. He accordingly at once set off for Blackfell Hollow, where he knew they were, accompanied by his eldest son and two of the farm-servants. The little Duke of Cheshire, who was perfectly frantic with anxiety, begged hard to be allowed to go too, but Mr. Otis would not allow him, as he was afraid there might be a scuffle. On arriving at the spot, however, he found that the gypsies had gone, and it was evident that their departure had been rather sudden, as the fire was still burning, and some plates were lying on the grass. Having sent off Washington and the two men to scour the district, he ran home, and dispatched telegrams to all the police inspectors in the county, telling them to look out for a little girl who had been kidnapped by tramps or gypsies. He then ordered his horse to be brought round, and after insisting on his wife and the three boys sitting down to dinner, rode off down the Ascot Road with a groom. He had hardly, however, gone a couple of miles when he heard somebody galloping after him, and, looking round, saw the little Duke coming up on his pony, with his face very flushed and no hat. "I'm awfully sorry, Mr. Otis," gasped out the boy, "but I can't eat any dinner as long as Virginia is lost. Please, don't be angry with me; if you had let us be engaged last year there would never have been all this trouble. You won't send me back, will you? I can't go! I won't go!"

The Minister could not help smiling at the handsome young scapegrace, and was a good deal touched at his devotion to Virginia, so leaning down from his horse, he patted him kindly on the shoulders, and said, "Well, Cecil, if you won't go back I suppose you must come with me, but I must get you a hat at Ascot."

"Oh, bother my hat! I want Virginia!" cried the little Duke, laughing, and they galloped on to the railway station. There Mr. Otis inquired of the stationmaster if anyone answering the description of Virginia had been seen on the platform, but could get no news of her. The stationmaster, however, wired up and down the line, and assured him that a strict watch would be kept for her, and, after having bought a hat for the little Duke from a linen draper, who was just putting up his shutters, Mr. Otis rode off to Bexley, a village about four miles away, which he was told was a well-known haunt of the gypsies, as there was a large common next to it. Here they roused up the rural policeman, but could get no information from him, and, after riding all over the common, they turned their horses' heads homewards, and reached the Chase about eleven o'clock, dead-tired and almost heart-broken. They found Washington and the twins waiting for them at the gate-house with lanterns, as the avenue was very dark. Not the slightest trace of Virginia had been discovered. The gypsies had been caught on Brockley meadows, but she was not with them, and they had explained their sudden departure by saying that they had mistaken the date of Chorton Fair, and had gone off in a hurry for fear they might be late. Indeed, they had been quite distressed at hearing of Virginia's disappearance, as they were very grateful to Mr. Otis for having allowed them to camp in his park, and four of their number had stayed behind to help in the search. The carp-pond had been dragged, and the whole Chase thoroughly gone over, but without any result. It was evident that, for that night, at any rate, Virginia was lost to them; and it was in a state of the deepest depression that Mr. Otis and the boys walked up to the house, the groom following behind with the two horses and the pony. In the hall they found a group of frightened servants, and lying on a sofa in the library was poor Mrs. Otis, almost out of her mind with terror and anxiety, and having her forehead bathed with eau-de-cologne by the old housekeeper. Mr. Otis at once insisted on her having something to eat, and ordered up supper for the whole party. It was a melancholy meal, as hardly anyone spoke, and even the twins were awe-struck, and subdued, as they were very fond of their sister. When they had finished, Mr. Otis, in spite of the entreaties of the little Duke, ordered them all to bed, saying that nothing more could be done that night, and that he would telegraph in the morning to Scotland Yard for some detectives to be sent down immediately. Just as they were passing out of the dining-room, midnight began to boom from the clock-tower, and when the last stroke sounded they heard a crash and a sudden shrill cry; a dreadful peal of thunder shook the house, a strain of unearthly music floated through the air, a panel at the top of the staircase flew back with a loud noise, and out on the landing, looking very pale and white, with a little casket in her hand, stepped Virginia. In a moment they had all rushed up to her. Mrs. Otis clasped her passionately in her arms, the Duke smoth-ered her with violent kisses, and the twins executed a wild war-dance round the group.

"Good heavens, child! Where have you been?" said Mr. Otis, rather angrily, thinking that she had been playing some foolish trick on them. "Cecil and I have been riding all over the country looking for you, and your mother has been frightened to death. You must never play these practical jokes anymore."

"Except on the Ghost! except on the Ghost!" shrieked the twins, as they capered about.

"My own darling, thank God you are found, you must never leave my side again," murmured Mrs. Otis, as she kissed the trembling child, and smoothed the tangled gold of her hair.

"Papa," said Virginia quietly, "I have been with the Ghost. He is dead, and you must come and see him. He had been very wicked, but he was really sorry for all that he had done, and he gave me this box of beautiful jewels before he died."

The whole family gazed at her in mute amazement, but

she was quite grave and serious; and, turning round, she led them through the opening in the wainscoting down a narrow secret corridor, Washington following with a lighted candle, which he had caught up from the table. Finally, they came to a great oak door, studded with rusty nails. When Virginia touched it, it swung back on its heavy hinges, and they found themselves in a little, low room, with a vaulted ceiling, and one tiny grated window. Imbedded in the wall was a huge iron ring, and chained to it was a gaunt skeleton, that was stretched out at full length on the stone floor, and seemed to be trying to grasp with its long, fleshless fingers an old-fashioned trencher and ewer, that were placed just out of its reach. The jug had evidently been once filled with water, as it was covered with green mould. There was nothing on the trencher but a pile of dust. Virginia knelt down beside the skeleton, and, folding her little hands together, began to pray silently, while the rest of the party looked on in wonder at the terrible tragedy whose secret was now disclosed to them.

"Hallo!" suddenly exclaimed one of the twins, who had been looking out of the window trying to discover in what wing of the house the room was situated. "Hallo! the old withered almond-tree has blossomed. I can see the flowers quite plainly in the moonlight."

"God has forgiven him," said Virginia gravely, as she rose to her feet, and a beautiful light seemed to illumine her face.

"What an angel you are!" cried the young Duke, and he put his arm around her neck and kissed her.

The Phantom Rickshaw

by Rudyard Kipling

Born in Bombay, India, on December 30, 1865, to a teacher and connoisseur of Indian art and a minister's daughter, RUDYARD KIPLING was raised mostly by nannies. After absorbing much of India's culture and spirit (he learned Hindustani simultaneously with English), he was sent to school in England.

Later, at the United Services College, Westward Ho, North Devon, he edited the college magazine but was not satisfied with his school experiences. So, in 1883, at the age of seventeen, he returned to his beloved India. There, his father used his influence to get Kipling on the staff of the Civil and Military Gazette. His work on the paper and his fictional writing during this time, including the novel Plain Tales from the Hills, published in 1887, constitute Kipling's first successes in print.

Another newspaper job sent Kipling back to England in 1889. There he met Caroline Starr Balestier, and three years later the two married and moved to Brattleboro, Vermont. That same year, 1892, Barrack-Room Ballads was published, and it remained Kipling's best known book until the publication of The Jungle Book in 1894.

Kipling and his family, two girls and a boy, returned to England in 1896 after he quarreled with his brother-in-law. Then, in 1898, on a trip to New York, Kipling lost his elder daughter to double pneumonia and nearly died himself.

In the early 1900s, after completing the highly successful novel Kim, Kipling devoted himself to political writings. His reputation grew rapidly in England, and in 1907 he received international acclaim when awarded the Nobel Prize for Literature. After an extremely active life in which he produced myriad articles, books, short stories, and even a few plays, Kipling died rather suddenly on January 18, 1936, at the age of seventy.

The "Phantom Rickshaw" demonstrates Kipling's penchant for horror as well as his remarkable talent for tale-telling. In this excerpt from the lengthy short story, a rejected woman dies of a broken heart and returns to seek revenge on her former lover.

Three years ago it was my fortune—my great misfortune—to sail from Gravesend to Bombay, on return from long leave, with one Agnes Keith-Wessington, wife of an officer on the Bombay side. It does not in the least concern you to know what manner of woman she was. Be content with the knowledge that, ere the voyage had ended, both she and I were desperately and unreasoningly in love with one another. Heaven knows that I can make the admission now without one particle of vanity. In matters of this sort there is always one who gives and another who accepts. From the first day of our ill-omened attachment, I was conscious that Agnes's passion was a stronger, a more dominant, and—if I may use the expression—a purer sentiment than mine. Whether she recognized the fact then, I do not know. Afterwards it was bitterly plain to both of us.

Arrived at Bombay in the spring of the year, we went our

respective ways, to meet no more for the next three or four months, when my leave and her love took us both to Simla. There we spent the season together; and there my fire of straw burnt itself out to a pitiful end with the closing year. I attempt no excuse. I make no apology. Mrs. Wessington had given up much for my sake, and was prepared to give up all. From my own lips, in August, 1882, she learnt that I was sick of her presence, tired of her company, and weary of the sound of her voice. Ninety-nine women out of a hundred would have wearied of me as I wearied of them; seventy-five of that number would have promptly avenged themselves by active and obtrusive flirtation with other men. Mrs. Wessington was the hundredth. On her neither my openly-expressed aversion, nor the cutting brutalities with which I garnished our interviews had the least effect.

"Jack, darling!" was her one eternal cuckoo-cry, "I'm sure it's all a mistake—a hideous mistake; and we'll be good friends again some day. *Please* forgive me, Jack, dear."

I was the offender, and I knew it. That knowledge transformed my pity into passive endurance, and, eventually, into blind hate—the same instinct, I suppose, which prompts a man to savagely stamp on the spider he has but half killed. And with this hate in my bosom the season of 1882 came to an end.

Next year we met again at Simla—she with her monotonous face and timid attempts at reconciliation, and I with loathing of her in every fiber of my frame. Several times I could not avoid meeting her alone; and on each occasion her words were identically the same. Still the unreasoning wail that it was all a "mistake"; and still the hope of eventually "making friends." I might have seen, had I cared to look, that that hope only was keeping her alive. She grew more wan and thin month by month. You will agree with me, at least, that such conduct would have driven anyone to despair. It was uncalled for, childish, unwomanly. I maintain that she was much to blame. But I could not have continued pretending to love her when I didn't, could I? It would have been unfair to us both.

Last year we met again—on the same terms as before. The same weary appeals, and the same curt answers from my lips. At least I would make her see how wholly wrong and hopeless were her attempts at resuming the old relationship. As the season wore on, we fell apart—that is to say, she found it difficult to meet me, for I had other and more absorbing interests to attend to. When I think it over quietly in my sick-room, the season of 1884 seems a confused nightmare wherein light and shade were fantastically intermingled—my courtship of little Kitty Mannering; my hopes, doubts, and fears; our long rides together; my trembling avowal of attachment; her reply; and now and again a vision of a white face flitting by in the rickshaw with the black and white liveries I once watched for so earnestly; the wave of Mrs. Wessington's gloved hand; and, when she met me alone, which was but seldom, the irksome monotony of her appeal. I loved Kitty Mannering, honestly, heartily loved her, and with my new love for her grew my hatred for Agnes. In August Kitty and I were engaged. The next day I met those accursed "magpie" *jhampanies* at the back of Jakko, and, moved by some passing sentiment of pity, stopped to tell Mrs. Wessington everything. She knew it already.

"So I hear you're engaged, Jack dear." Then, without a moment's pause: "I'm sure it's all a mistake—a hideous mistake. We shall be as good friends some day, Jack, as we ever were."

My answer would have made even a man wince. It cut the dying woman before me like the blow of a whip. "Please forgive me, Jack; I didn't mean to make you angry; but it's true, it's true!"

And Mrs. Wessington broke down completely. I turned away and left her to finish her journey in peace, feeling, but only for a moment or two, that I had been an unutterably mean hound. I looked back, and saw that she had turned her rickshaw with the idea, I suppose, of overtaking me. She was holding her handkerchief in her left hand and was leaning back exhausted against the rickshaw cushions. I turned my horse up a bypath near the Sanjowlie Reservoir and literally ran away. Once I fancied I heard a faint call of "Jack!" This may have been imagination. I never stopped to verify it. Ten minutes later I came across Kitty on horseback; and, in the delight of a long ride with her, forgot all about the interview.

A week later Mrs. Wessington died, and the inexpressible burden of her existence was removed from my life. I went Plainsward perfectly happy. Before three months were over I had forgotten all about her. At the beginning of April of this year, 1885, I was at Simla—semi-deserted Simla—once more, and was deep in lover's talks and walks with Kitty. It was decided that we should be married at the end of June.

Fourteen delightful days passed almost before I noticed their flight. Then, aroused to the sense of what was proper among mortals circumstanced as we were, I pointed out to Kitty that an engagement ring was the outward and visible sign of her dignity as an engaged girl; and that she must forthwith come to Hamilton's to be measured for one. To Hamilton's we accordingly went on the 15th of April, 1885. Remember that—whatever my doctor may say to the contrary—I was then in perfect health, enjoying a well-balanced mind and an absolutely tranquil spirit. Kitty and I entered Hamilton's shop together, and there, regardless of the order of affairs, I measured Kitty's finger for the ring in the presence of the amused assistant. We then rode out down the slope that leads to the Combermere Bridge and Peliti's shop.

While my Waler was cautiously feeling his way over the loose shale, and Kitty was laughing and chattering at my side—while all Simla, that is to say as much of it as had then come from the Plains, was grouped round the Reading-room and Peliti's veranda—I was aware that someone, apparently at a vast distance, was calling me by my Christian name. It struck me that I had heard the voice before, but when and where I could not at once determine. In the short space it took to cover the road between the path from Hamilton's shop and the first plank of the Combermere Bridge I had thought over half-a-dozen people who might have committed such a solecism, and had eventually decided that it must have been some singing in my ears. Immediately opposite Peliti's shop my eye was arrested by the sight of four *jhampanies* in black and white livery, pulling a yellow-paneled, cheap, bazaar rickshaw. In a moment my mind flew back to the previous season and Mrs. Wessington with a sense of irritation and disgust. Was it not enough that the woman was dead and done with, without her black and white servitors reappearing to spoil the day's happiness? Whoever employed them now, I thought I would call upon, and ask as a personal favor to change her *jhampanies'* livery.

"Kitty," I cried, "there are poor Mrs. Wessington's *jham-panies* turned up again! I wonder who has them now?"

Kitty had known Mrs. Wessington slightly last season,

and had always been interested in the sickly woman. "What? Where?" she asked. "I can't see them anywhere."

Even as she spoke, her horse, swerving from a laden mule, threw himself directly in front of the advancing rickshaw. I had scarcely time to utter a word of warning when, to my unutterable horror, horse and rider passed *through* men and carriage as if they had been thin air.

"What's the matter?" cried Kitty. "What made you call out so foolishly, Jack? There was lots of space between the mule and the veranda, and if you think I can't ride—There!"

Whereupon willful Kitty set off, her dainty little head in the air, at a hand-gallop in the direction of the old bandstand; fully expecting, as she herself afterwards told me, that I should follow her. What was the matter? Nothing, indeed. Either that I was mad, or drunk, or that Simla was haunted with devils. I reined in my impatient cob, and turned round. The rickshaw had turned too, and now stood immediately facing me, near the left railing of the Combermere Bridge.

"Jack! Jack darling." (There was no mistake about the words this time: they rang through my brain as if they had been shouted in my ear.) "It's some hideous mistake, I'm sure. *Please* forgive me, Jack, and let's be friends again."

The rickshaw hood had fallen back, and inside, as I hope and daily pray for the death I dread by night, sat Mrs. Keith-Wessington, handkerchief in hand, and golden head bowed on her breast.

How long I stared motionless I do not know. Finally, I was aroused by my groom taking the Waler's bridle and asking whether I was ill. I tumbled off my horse and dashed, half fainting, into Peliti's for a glass of cherry brandy. There, two or three couples were gathered round the coffee tables discussing the gossip of the day. Their trivialities were more comforting to me just then than the consolations of religion could have been. I plunged into the midst of the conversation at once; chatted, laughed and jested with a face (when I caught a glimpse of it in a mirror) as white and drawn as that of the corpse. Three or four men noticed my condition; and, evidently setting it down to the results of over many pegs, charitably endeavored to draw me apart from the rest of the loungers. But I refused to be led away. I must have talked for about ten minutes or so, though it seemed an eternity to me, when I heard Kitty's clear voice outside inquiring for me. In another minute she had entered the shop, prepared to roundly upbraid me for failing so signally in my duties. Something in my face stopped her.

"Why, Jack," she cried, "what *have* you been doing? What *has* happened? Are you ill?" Thus driven into a direct lie, I said that the sun had been a little too much for me. It was close upon five o'clock of a cloudy April afternoon, and the sun had been hidden all day. I saw my mistake as soon as the words were out of my mouth; I attempted to recover it, blundered hopelessly, and followed Kitty, in a regal rage, out of doors, amid the smiles of my acquaintances. I made some excuse (I have forgotten what) on the score of my feeling faint; and cantered away to my hotel, leaving Kitty to finish the ride by herself.

In my room I sat down and tried calmly to reason out the matter. Here was I, Theobald Jack Pansay, a well-educated Bengal civilian in the year of grace 1885, presumably sane, certainly healthy, driven in terror from my sweetheart's side by the apparition of a woman who had been dead and buried eight months ago. These were facts that I could not blink.

Nothing was further from my thought than any memory of Mrs. Wessington when Kitty and I left Hamilton's shop. Nothing was more utterly commonplace than the stretch of wall opposite Peliti's. It was broad daylight. The road was full of people; and yet here, look you, in defiance of every law of probability, in direct outrage of Nature's ordinance, there had appeared to me a face from the grave.

Kitty's Arab had gone *through* the rickshaw; so that my first hope that some woman marvelously like Mrs. Wessington had hired the carriage and the coolies with their old livery was lost. Again and again I went round this tread-mill of thought; and again and again gave up baffled in despair.

Next morning I sent a penitent note to Kitty, imploring her to overlook my strange conduct of the previous after-noon. My Divinity was still very wroth, and a personal apol-ogy was necessary. I explained, with a fluency born of night-long pondering over a falsehood, that I had been attacked with a sudden palpitation of the heart—the result of indigestion. This eminently practical solution had its effect; and Kitty and I rode out that afternoon with the shadow of my first lie dividing us.

Nothing would please her save a canter round Jakko. With my nerves still unstrung from the previous night I fee-bly protested against the notion, suggesting Observatory Hill, Jutogh, the Boleaugunge road—anything rather than the Jakko round. Kitty was angry and a little hurt, so I yielded from fear of provoking further misunderstanding, and we set out together towards Chota Simla. The wretched horses appeared to fly, and my heart beat quicker and quicker as we neared the crest of the ascent. My mind had been full of Mrs. Wessington all the afternoon; and every inch of the Jakko road bore witness to our old-time walks and talks.

As a fitting climax, in the middle of the level men call the Ladies' Mile, the Horror was awaiting me. No other rickshaw was in sight—only the four black and white *jhampanies*, the yellow-paneled carriage, and the golden head of the woman within—all apparently just as I had left them eight months and one fortnight ago! For an instant I fancied that Kitty must see what I saw—we were so marvelously sympathetic in all things. Her next words undeceived me—"Not a soul in sight! Come along, Jack, and I'll race you to the Reservoir buildings!" Her wiry little Arab was off like a bird, my Waler following close behind, and in this order we dashed under the cliffs. Half a minute brought us within fifty yards of the rickshaw. I pulled my Waler and fell back a little. The rickshaw was directly in the middle of the road; and once more the Arab passed through it, my horse following. "Jack, Jack dear! *Please* forgive me," rang with a wail in my ears, and, after an interval, "It's all a mistake, a hideous mistake!"

I spurred my horse like a man possessed. When I turned my head at the Reservoir works the black and white liveries were still waiting—patiently waiting—under the gray hillside, and the wind brought me a mocking echo of the words I had just heard. Kitty bantered me a good deal on my silence throughout the remainder of the ride.

I was to dine with the Mannerings that night and had barely time to canter home to dress. On the road to Elysium Hill I overheard two men talking together in the dusk—"It's a curious thing," said one, "how completely all trace of it disappeared. You know, my wife was insanely fond of the woman (never could see anything in her myself) and wanted me to pick up her old rickshaw and coolies if they were to be got for

love or money. Would you believe that the man she hired it from tells me that all four of the men, they were brothers, died of cholera, on the way to Hardwar, poor devils; and the rickshaw has been broken up by the man himself. Told me he never used a dead *Memsahib's* rickshaw. Spoilt his luck. Queer notion, wasn't it? Fancy poor little Mrs. Wessington spoiling any one's luck but her own!" I laughed aloud at this point, and my laugh jarred on me as I uttered it. So there *were* ghosts of rickshaws after all, and ghostly employments in the other world!

Then I saw the infernal thing blocking my path in the twilight. Some malignant devil entered into me that evening, for I have a dim recollection of talking the commonplaces of the day for five minutes to the thing in front of me.

"Mad as a hatter, poor devil—or drunk. Max, try and get him to come home."

Surely *that* was not Mrs. Wessington's voice! The two men had overheard me speaking to the empty air and had returned to look after me. They were very kind and consider-ate, and from their words evidently gathered that I was extremely drunk. I thanked them confusedly and cantered away to my hotel, there changed, and arrived at the Mannerings' ten minutes late. I pleaded the darkness of the night as an excuse; was rebuked by Kitty for my unlover-like tardiness; and sat down.

The conversation had already become general; and, under cover of it, I was addressing some tender small talk to my sweetheart when I was aware that at the further end of the table a short red-whiskered man was describing with much broidery his encounter with a mad unknown that evening. A few sentences convinced me that he was repeating the incident of half an hour ago. In the middle of the story he looked round for applause, as professional storytellers do, caught my eye, and straightway collapsed. There was a moment's awkward silence, and the red-whiskered man muttered something to the effect that he had "forgotten the rest," thereby sacrificing a reputation as a good storyteller which he had built up for six seasons past. I blessed him from the bottom of my heart and—went on with my fish.

In the fullness of time that dinner came to an end, and with genuine regret, I tore myself away from Kitty—as certain as I was of my own existence that It would be waiting for me outside the door. The red-whiskered man, who had been introduced to me as Dr. Heatherlegh of Simla, volunteered to bear me company as far as our roads lay together. I accepted his offer with gratitude.

My instinct had not deceived me. It lay in readiness in the Mall. The red-whiskered man went to the point at once, in a manner that showed he had been thinking over it all dinner time.

"I say, Pansay, what the deuce was the matter with you this evening on the Elysium road?" The suddenness of the question wrenched an answer from me before I was aware.

"That!" said I, pointing to It.

"*That* may be either *D.T.* or eyes for aught I know. Now you don't liquor. I saw as much at dinner, so it can't be *D.T.* There's nothing whatever where you're pointing, though you're sweating and trembling with fright like a scared pony. Therefore, I conclude that it's eyes. And I ought to understand all about them. Come along home with me. I'm on the Blessington lower road."

To my intense delight the rickshaw, instead of waiting for

us, kept about twenty yards ahead—and this, too, whether we walked, trotted, or cantered. In the course of that long night ride I had told my companion almost as much as I have told you here.

"Well, you've spoilt one of the best tales I've ever laid tongue to," said he, "but I'll forgive you for the sake of what you've gone through. Now come home and do what I tell you; and when I've cured you, young man, let this be a lesson to you to steer clear of women and indigestible food till the day of your death."

The rickshaw kept steadily in front; and my red-whiskered friend seemed to derive great pleasure from my account of its exact whereabouts.

"Eyes, Pansay—all eyes, brain and stomach; and the greatest of these three is stomach. You've too much conceited brain, too little stomach, and thoroughly unhealthy eyes. Get your stomach straight and the rest follows. I'll take sole medical charge of you from this hour, for you're too interesting a phenomenon to be passed over."

His attempts towards my cure commenced almost immediately, and for a week I never left his sight. Many a time in the course of that week did I bless the good fortune which had thrown me in contact with Simla's best and kindest doctor. Day by day my spirits grew lighter and more equable. Day by day, too, I became more and more inclined to fall in with Heatherlegh's "spectral illusion" theory, implicating eyes, brain, and stomach. I wrote to Kitty, telling her that a slight sprain caused by a fall from my horse kept me indoors for a few days; and that I should be recovered before she had time to regret my absence.

At the end of the week Heatherlegh dismissed me as

brusquely as he had taken charge of me. Here is his parting benediction: "Man, I certify to your mental cure, and that's as much as to say I've cured most of your bodily ailments. Now, get your traps out of this as soon as you can; and be off to make love to Miss Kitty."

I was endeavoring to express my thanks for his kindness. He cut me short. "Now, go out and see if you can find the eyes-brain-and-stomach business again. I'll give you a lakh for each time you see it."

Half an hour later I was in the Mannerings' drawing-room with Kitty—drunk with the intoxication of present happiness and the foreknowledge that I should never more be troubled with Its hideous presence. Strong in the sense of my new-found security, I proposed to take a ride at once; and, by preference, a canter round Jakko.

Never have I felt so well, so overladen with vitality and mere animal spirits as I did on the afternoon of the 30th of April. Kitty was delighted at the change in my appearance, and complimented me on it in her delightfully frank and out-spoken manner. We left the Mannerings' house together, laughing and talking, and cantered along the Chota Simla road as of old.

I was in haste to reach the Sanjowlie Reservoir and there make my assurance doubly sure. We were just below the Convent, and from sheer wantonness I was making my Waler plunge and curvet across the road as I tickled it with the loop of my riding-whip.

We had rounded the corner above the Convent; and a few yards further on could see across to Sanjowlie. In the center of the level road stood the black and white liveries, the yellow-paneled rickshaw and Mrs. Keith-Wessington. I pulled up, looked, rubbed my eyes, and, I believe, must have said some-thing. The next thing I knew was that I was lying face down-ward on the road, with Kitty kneeling above me in tears.

"Has it gone, child?" I gasped. Kitty only wept more bitterly.

"Has what gone? Jack dear, what does it all mean? There must be a mistake somewhere, Jack. A hideous mistake." Her last words brought me to my feet—mad—raving for the time being.

"Yes, there *is* a mistake somewhere," I repeated, "a hideous mistake. Come and look at It!"

I have an indistinct idea that I dragged Kitty by the wrist along the road up to where It stood, and implored her for pity's sake to speak to it, to tell It that we were betrothed! that neither Death nor Hell could break the tie between us; and Kitty only knows how much more to the same effect. Now and again I appealed passionately to the Terror in the rickshaw to bear witness to all I had said, and to release me from a torture that was killing me. As I talked I suppose I must have told Kitty of my old relations with Mrs. Wessington, for I saw her listen intently with white face and blazing eyes.

"Thank you, Mr. Pansay," she said, "that's *quite* enough. Bring my horse."

The grooms had come up with the recaptured horses; and as Kitty sprang into her saddle I caught hold of the bridle entreating her to hear me out and forgive. My answer was the cut of her riding whip across my face from mouth to eye, and a word or two of farewell that even now I cannot write down. So I judged, and judged rightly, that Kitty knew all; and I stag-gered back to the side of the rickshaw. I had no self-respect.

Just then, Heatherlegh, who must have been following Kitty and me at a distance, cantered up.

"Doctor," I said, pointing to my face, "here's Miss Mannering's signature to my order of dismissal and . . . I'll thank you for that lakh as soon as convenient."

"I'll stake my professional reputation—" he began.

"Don't be a fool," I whispered. "I've lost my life's happiness and you'd better take me home."

Seven days later I was aware that I was lying in Heatherlegh's room as weak as a child. Heatherlegh was watching me intently from behind the papers on his writing table. His first words were not very encouraging; but I was too far spent to be much moved by them.

"Here's Miss Kitty has sent back your letters. Here's a packet that looks like a ring, and a cheerful sort of a note from Mannering Papa, which I've taken the liberty of reading and burning. The old gentleman's not pleased with you."

"And Kitty?" I asked dully.

"Rather more drawn than her father from what she says. By the same token you must have been letting out any number of queer reminiscences just before I met you. Says that a man who would have behaved to a woman as you did to Mrs. Wessington ought to kill himself out of sheer pity for his kind. She's a hot-headed little virago, your mash. Says she'll die before she ever speaks to you again."

I groaned and turned over on the other side.

"Now you've got your choice, my friend. This engagement has to be broken off; and the Mannerings don't want to be too hard on you. Was it broken through *D.T.* or epileptic fits? Say the word and I'll tell 'em it's fits. Come! I'll give you five minutes to think over it."

During those five minutes, I believe that I explored thoroughly the lowest circles of the Inferno which it is permitted man to tread on earth. And at the same time I myself was watching myself faltering through the dark labyrinths of doubt, misery, and utter despair. I wondered, as Heatherlegh in his chair might have wondered, which dreadful alternative I should adopt. Presently I heard myself answering in a voice that I hardly recognized. "They're confoundedly particular about morality in these parts. Give 'em fits, Heatherlegh, and my love. Now let me sleep a bit longer."

Then my two selves joined, and it was only I (half crazed, devil-driven I) that tossed in my bed, tracing step by step the history of the past month.

"Why couldn't Agnes have left me alone? I never did her any harm. It might just as well have been me as Agnes. Only I'd never have come back on purpose to kill *her*. Why can't I be left alone—left alone and happy?"

Next day I could not leave my bed. Heatherlegh told me in the morning that he had received an answer from Mr. Mannering, and that, thanks to his (Heatherlegh's) friendly offices, the story of my affliction had traveled through the length and breadth of Simla, where I was on all sides much pitied.

"And that's rather more than you deserve," he concluded pleasantly, "though the Lord knows you've been going through a pretty severe mill. Never mind; we'll cure you yet, you perverse phenomenon."

I declined firmly to be cured. "You've been much too good to me already, old man," said I; "but I don't think I need trouble you further."

In my heart I knew that nothing Heatherlegh could do

would lighten the burden that had been laid upon me.

With that knowledge came also a sense of hopeless, impotent rebellion against the unreasonableness of it all. There were scores of men no better than I whose punishments had at least been reserved for another world and I felt that it was bitterly, cruelly unfair that I alone should have been singled out for so hideous a fate. This mood would in time give place to another where it seemed that the rickshaw and I were the only realities in a world of shadows; that Kitty was a ghost; that Mannering, Heatherlegh, and all the other men and women I knew were all ghosts. From mood to mood I tossed backwards and forwards for seven weary days, my body growing daily stronger and stronger, until the bedroom looking-glass told me that I had returned to everyday life and was as other men once more.

On the 15th of May, I left Heatherlegh's house at eleven o'clock in the morning; and the instinct of the bachelor drove me to the Club. There I found that every man knew my story as told by Heatherlegh, and was, in clumsy fashion, abnormally kind and attentive. Nevertheless, I recognized that for the rest of my natural life I should be among, but not of, my fellows; and I envied very bitterly indeed the laughing coolies on the Mall below. I lunched at the Club, and at four o'clock wandered aimlessly down the Mall in the vague hope of meeting Kitty. Close to the bandstand, the black and white liveries joined me; and I heard Mrs. Wessington's old appeal at my side. I had been expecting this ever since I came out, and was only surprised at her delay. The phantom rickshaw and I went side by side along the Chota Simla road in silence. Close to the bazaar, Kitty and a man on horseback overtook and passed us. For any sign she gave, I might have been a dog in the road. So Kitty and her companion, and I and my ghostly Light-o'-Love, crept round Jakko in couples.

Once more I wearily climbed the Convent slope and entered the level road. Here, Kitty and the man started off at a canter, and I was left alone with Mrs. Wessington. "Agnes," said I, "will you put back your hood and tell me what it all means?" The hood dropped noiselessly and I was face to face with my dead and buried mistress. She was wearing the dress in which I had last seen her alive; carried the same tiny hand-kerchief in her right hand; and the same card-case in her left. (A woman eight months dead with a card-case!)

"Agnes," I repeated, "for pity's sake tell me what it all means." Mrs. Wessington leant forward, with that odd, quick turn of the head I used to know so well, and spoke.

If my story had not already so madly overleaped the bounds of all human belief, I should apologize to you now. As I know that no one—no, not even Kitty, for whom it is writ-ten as some sort of justification of my conduct—will believe me, I will go on. Mrs. Wessington spoke, and I walked with her from the Sanjowlie road to the turning below the Commander-in-Chief's house as I might walk by the side of any living woman's rickshaw, deep in conversation.

There had been a garden-party at the Commander-in-Chief's, and we two joined the crowd of homeward-bound folk. As I saw them then it seemed that *they* were the shad-ows—impalpable fantastic shadows—that divided for Mrs. Wessington's rickshaw to pass through. What we said dur-ing the course of that weird interview I cannot—indeed, I dare not—tell. It was a ghastly and yet in some indefinable way a marvelously dear experience. Could it be possible, I wondered, that I was in this life to woo a second time the woman I had killed by my own neglect and cruelty?

I met Kitty on the homeward road—a shadow among shadows.

If I were to describe all the incidents of the next fortnight in their order, my story would never come to an end; and your patience would be exhausted. Morning after morning and evening after evening, the ghostly rickshaw and I used to wander through Simla together. More than once I have walked down the Mall deep in conversation with Mrs. Wessington to the unspeakable amazement of the passersby.

Before I had been out and about a week, I learnt that the "fit" theory had been discarded in favor of insanity. However, I made no change in my mode of life. I called, rode, and dined out as freely as ever. I had a passion for the society of my kind which I had never felt before; I hungered to be among the realities of life; and at the same time I felt vaguely unhappy when I had been separated too long from my ghostly companion. It would be almost impossible to describe my varying moods from the 15th of May up to today.

The presence of the rickshaw filled me by turns with horror, blind fear, a dim sort of pleasure, and utter despair. I dared not leave Simla; and I knew that my stay there was killing me. I knew, moreover, that it was my destiny to die slowly and a little every day. By day I wandered with Mrs. Wessington, almost content. By night I implored Heaven to let me return to the world as I used to know it. Above all these varying moods lay the sensation of dull, numbing wonder that the seen and the unseen should mingle so strangely on this earth to hound one poor soul to its grave.

∞

August 27th—Heatherlegh has been indefatigable in his attendance on me; and only yesterday told me that I ought to send in an application for sick-leave. An application to escape the company of a phantom! Heatherlegh's proposition moved me to almost hysterical laughter. I told him that I should await the end quietly at Simla; and I am sure that the end is not far off. Believe me that I dread its advent more than any word can say; and I torture myself nightly with a thousand speculations as to the manner of my death.

Shall I die in my bed decently and as an English gentleman should die; or, in one last walk on the Mall, will my soul be wrenched from me to take its place for ever and ever by the side of that ghastly phantasm? Shall I return to my old lost allegiance in the next world, or shall I meet Agnes loathing her and bound to her side through all eternity?

As the day of my death draws nearer, the intense horror that all living flesh feels towards escaped spirits from beyond the grave grows more and more powerful. It is an awful thing to go down quick among the dead with scarcely one half of your life completed. It is a thousand times more awful to wait as I do in your midst, for I know not what unimaginable terror. Pity me, at least on the score of my "delusion," for I know you will never believe what I have written here. Yet as surely as ever a man was done to death by the Powers of Darkness, I am that man.

In justice, too, pity her. For as surely as ever woman was killed by man, I killed Mrs. Wessington. And the last portion of my punishment is even now upon me.

GLOSSARY

arquebus–a variation of the word *harquebus*, which was a portable gun, invented in the 15th century, that was so heavy it had to be fired from a support

baleful–menacing; threatening evil

bogies–ghosts

charnel-house–a place in which corpses are deposited

colleen–an Irish girl

cryptograph–a system of secret writing

dimity–a thin cotton fabric woven with stripes or checks

draying–hauling goods

ewer–a pitcher or jug with a wide spout

falchion–a broad, short sword

fugacious–fleeting, transitory

gyves–shackles, especially for the legs

heliotrope–a plant with small, fragrant, purple flowers

jhampanies–a kind of sedan chair carried by four men (primarily used in the hill country of India)

lakh–Indian money, the sum of 100,000 rupees

lares et penates–the cherished possessions of a family or household

liveries–uniforms worn by servants

mash–sweetheart

mignonette–plant with clusters of small, fragrant, greenish-white flowers with orange centers

Memsahib–a term of respect for a married European woman

perdition–a state of final spiritual ruin

peripatetic–walking or traveling about

phantasmata–apparitions and ghosts

portmanteau–suitcase

sang froid–coolness of mind, calmness

sanguineous–pertaining to blood

scapegrace–a persistent rascal

surfeited–excessively indulgent, as with overeating

trencher–a flat piece of wood on which food is served